AN UNEXPECTED GIFT

A HOT DAM HOMES HOLIDAY NOVELLA

HARPER ROBSON

2022

Contents

Cover Design by Cate Ashwood at *Ashwood Designs*

Additional Cover Design by *100 Covers*

Editing by Sandra and Julia at One Love Editing

Updated: 4.22.2025

CHAPTER ONE

MATTHEW

One Year Ago

My head pounds like someone's operating a jackhammer behind my eyes as I walk into the hotel bar. The smooth jazz playing softly over the sound system is oddly soothing and the pain in my head eases slightly as I pause, letting my eyes adjust to the lower lighting. The wall behind the bar is brick, and there are industrial accents throughout the space, but the furniture is soft and inviting. Plush chairs are gathered around low tables, and flickering votive candles cast a warm glow throughout the space.

"Make yourself comfortable anywhere you like. I'll be right over to take your order." A pretty young server smiles at me as she passes by with a tray of drinks.

I hadn't intended to stay at the office so late, but unsurprisingly, I got sucked into a project and lost track of the time.

Making my way over to a quiet corner, I settle into one of the low couches and look around. Set off to one side of the hotel lobby, the lounge has a welcoming vibe, like most places in Chicago.

As soon as I'm settled, the server approaches and I order an expensive whiskey and some appetizers. It's not exactly a doctor-recommended strategy, but I'm hoping a little alcohol will help me fall asleep faster. If the stars all align, maybe I'll even sleep through the night.

Sinking back into the comfortable seat, I pull out my phone out of habit. Michele hasn't texted since there's really no reason to. I'm just so accustomed to checking for messages from her, it feels strange not to. She told me before I left on this trip that she's already found a condo, so when I get home, her things will already be moved out. I understand why she wants to cut the cord, and she's probably right, but it still stings. After more than two decades, three kids and building a multi-million-dollar company, she's finally had enough of playing second fiddle to whatever else is going on my life. She has rightly decided she deserves more than what I've been giving her. Can't blame her for that.

Before I can sink too far into those moody thoughts, my drink arrives, so I waste no time taking a sip, closing my eyes to let the smoke and vanilla flavor spread over my tongue.

When I open them, my gaze is drawn to an attractive guy at the bar. He's younger than me, maybe in his mid-thirties, with thick, sandy blond hair that flops carelessly over his forehead. When the bartender asks him a question, I notice his broad shoulders as he leans in to answer. He's got the all-American good looks of a Texas high school quarterback, and the easy way interacts with people around him suggests the kind of confidence you get from living your entire life as one of the 'beautiful people'. One of those people who everyone else either wants to be with, or just wants to be.

The server comes by with my selection of small plates, so I order another whiskey, and when she walks away, I'm surprised to find my mystery man staring right back at me.

He's wearing a well-cut blue dress shirt, and there's a suit jacket thrown casually over the back of his barstool. He says a few more words to the bartender, and then turns back to me. Caught staring, I flash him a sheepish smile, averting my eyes quickly and taking a drink.

Looking up a moment later, I'm shocked to find him standing beside my table, his icy blue eyes trained on me. Now that he's closer, I can see he's probably closer to my age than I first thought; the laugh lines around his eyes betray his age, although he still gives off the vibe of a thirty-something. He gives me a friendly smile, and his eyes crinkle up at the corners. *He must laugh a lot.* Suddenly I have this vivid image of myself making him laugh, then grabbing him and planting tiny little mini kisses on those laugh lines. *Jesus, what the hell is in this Scotch?*

"Hi there," his deep voice is almost like gravel. "I noticed you seem to look exactly how I feel right now, like you've been 'rode hard and put away wet', so I thought I'd offer to buy you a friendly drink." He gives me a slightly crooked smile.

"Oh, um, I- ah" I stutter. *Smooth, Matthew.* Is he trying to pick me up? Am I giving off some kind of gay vibe right now? I'm not gay, but my body is responding to this man, and I don't know why. It feels weird. Oddly, it's also sort of thrilling, since I haven't felt this sort of physical pull to anyone for a long time, man or woman.

"Sure, why not?" I finally say, right as my lack of response is heading toward awkward territory.

He holds out his hand for me to shake "I'm Case," he says with a smile that makes my insides flutter.

"Nice to meet you, I'm Matt," I say, shaking his hand. "Have a seat."

He settles into the low couch across from me. "So, I assume you're from out of town too, since we're in a hotel bar?" he grins, taking a sip from his drink.

"You would assume correctly," I return his grin. "I'm heading home to Seattle tomorrow. Yourself?"

"San Diego," Case says. "I'm here for a conference, and there's one day left, but I think I might play hooky tomorrow. I'd forgotten how great this city is."

"I know, I love Chicago too," I smile sincerely. "Great food everywhere, friendly people; what more can you ask for?"

"Well, I could ask for better weather." Case grins. "I grew up in California, so I prefer snow stay in the mountains where it belongs. I'm happy to ski on it, but I don't love the driving in it." We both chuckle.

We make small talk for a while, and I learn he's a psychological researcher, running a study on mental health in LGBTQ youth, and he's been in Chicago presenting some of his preliminary findings at a conference.

"That sounds fascinating," I say, impressed. "I work with a game development studio. It's fun, but there's no life-saving research happening on my watch." I never offer the information that I actually own the studio. We've grown big enough that even people who know nothing about video games are aware of us, and it always leads to lots of work questions. It's usually great, but tonight, I don't want to be 'Matthew

Cartwright, successful tech entrepreneur'. I want a night off from worrying about how every move I make could reflect on the company. I just want to be Matt; a guy looking to have a good time and see where the night leads him.

Case is easy to talk to, and it's impossible for me to ignore the way my body is responding to him. I've always been able to appreciate physically attractive guys, but this visceral reaction I'm having is something else again. I'm not sure I've ever reacted to anyone this way. Before I realize it, we've been talking for several hours, and I might have had too much Scotch. That's the only reasonable explanation for the increasingly explicit images of the two of us together that keep popping into my head.

Michele and I got married young, right after college, and we missed out on a lot of things our friends got to experience. When we divorced, we talked about wanting to experience some of those things now, in a whole 'better late than never' philosophy. I chuckle to myself, since somehow I don't think fucking a stranger in a hotel room is what either of us had in mind, but hell, what do I have to lose? I'm a newly single, successful,

40-something. Maybe I should let myself have this experience. Does that mean I'm gay? I don't think so, but I don't think I care if it does. The chemistry between Case and me is just about impossible to resist. Truthfully, I'm not even sure I want to.

CHAPTER TWO

CASE

E ven in the dim light of the hotel lounge, the man sitting across from me takes my breath away. On their own, none of his features are all that striking, but put together, they create a face I can't seem to stop looking at. His full lips are slightly parted, and every so often he darts the tip of his tongue out to moisten them. His chocolate brown eyes are almost too big for his face, but when he turns them on me, I feel like he's got me pinned under a microscope. It's like he can see things in me no one else can. I know that sounds ridiculous, but I can't think of another way to describe it.

This guy has me hot and bothered in a way I haven't felt for a very long time.

I don't even know how long we've been sitting here, but I suddenly realize we're the last two in the bar. As much as I'm enjoying talking with Matt, what I would enjoy even more is getting him upstairs to my suite and peeling him out of his gorgeous suit so I can have my very wicked way with him.

"So," I say, leaning forward and catching his eye. "Looks like we're the last two party animals closing this place down. Would you be interested in... getting out of here?" I lick my lips slowly, my meaning unmistakable. "My suite is on the 30th floor. It's got a great view." I nearly laugh out loud at the ridiculous line, because if he thinks I'm actually inviting him upstairs to admire the view, we are definitely not on the same page. I normally have a little more game, but I'm strangely nervous. I *really* want him to say yes, and I realize I'm holding my breath while I wait for him to answer.

Matt freezes, a look of panic running across his face before he quickly schools his expression back to neutral. There's an awkward pause, and for a second I'm certain he's going to give me the brush off, but he sucks in a deep breath and squares his shoulders.

"Yeah. I'm interested. Let's go," he says, and I can feel the smile spread across my face at the same time as heat and liquid desire pool down low in my belly.

We make our way to the elevator in silence after taking care of the tab, and I can feel the tension rolling off him. He mentioned he was going through a divorce earlier, and I don't want to put pressure on him. Just before we get to my floor, I touch his forearm gently. His breath catches, and he turns to look at me. Those eyes... fuck, I want to drown in his eyes. I can see how nervous he is, but he's also incredibly turned on if his dilated pupils and rapid breathing are any sign.

"Hey, it's okay," I say softly. I search his face for any sign that he wants an out, but I don't find one. "If you're not into this, we don't have to-" His eyes go wide.

"No! No, it's fine," he says, closing his eyes and scrubbing a hand down his face before rubbing the back of his neck, looking down. "I'm sorry, it's.. been a while is all. I guess that's obvious." He gives an embarrassed laugh, and color creeps up the sides of his neck.

"Hey," I say again, waiting until he meets my eyes before speaking. "Don't worry, I'm going to take care of you, Matt. Is that okay?" That must have been what he needed to hear, because his shoulders relax, and he nods wordlessly as the elevator dings.

Somehow I get us inside my suite without dropping the damn keycard, and I'm hoping he didn't notice how much my hands were shaking. I have no idea what's making me so nervous; hooking up is pretty much my whole way of life, and I'm *never* nervous about it. But there's something about Matt that has me feeling off center.

Once we're inside, he walks over to the floor to ceiling windows. "Oh, wow," he murmurs as he takes in the city lights. It really is a spectacular view, but that's not what I'm interested in at the moment. I kick the door shut and stand behind him, close enough that I can feel his body heat even through our clothes. Reaching out, I slide both my hands around his waist so they're flat against his abs. Pressing up against his back, he sucks in a sharp breath as I gently graze my nose along the side of his neck. I let my breath flit across his heated skin while I press firmly against him.

"Do you like the view?" I whisper against the skin just behind his ear, then flicking his earlobe with my tongue. His quiet gasp and shiver tell me he's just as eager for this as I am. Continuing my slow perusal of his neck, I feel like I can smell his arousal. When I finally place my mouth at the place where his neck joins his collarbone and suck, he lets out a moan and I thrust my hips into him so he can feel how hard I am.

He turns in my arms to face me, and I grab his hips, hauling him in close as I grind my mouth onto his. I can taste the scotch on his lips, and he smells vaguely of sandalwood from his soap or cologne or something. As I walk him backwards, he clumsily unbuttons his shirt, and shucks it off his shoulders just as I get him backed up against the glass window. He sucks in a breath, arching his back as his warm skin makes contact with the cold glass. I chuckle. "Too cold for me to fuck you against the glass?" I whisper. "Because I have this vision of turning you around, holding your hands above your head and fucking you until you scream."

He groans, a shudder rolling through him.

"Or maybe," I continue, moving my hips against his, "I want you on your back, so I can see your face while I fuck you so hard you feel me in your throat."

He shivers, and starts kissing me even more frantically, fumbling awkwardly with my belt until I cover his hands with mine. Realizing he must not have a lot of experience with hooking up, my confidence returns. If there's one thing I know how to do, it's take charge in the bedroom.

"Matt," I whisper, and he looks up at me, his big eyes filled with uncertainty.

"I'm sorry," he starts, but I place a finger to his lips and smile.

"I said I want to take care of you tonight. Will you let me do that?" I whisper.

He swallows again, and I watch his Adam's apple move before he nods without a word.

I move his hands away from my belt and pull him into me for a gentle kiss, slowing things down for him. A leisurely fuck isn't exactly what I had in mind for tonight, but slow can be fun if you do it right.

Holding one of his hands, I turn to lead him into the bedroom, where we stand at the foot of the bed.

Slowly, I undo the buttons of his dress shirt, bringing him in close to me as I push it off his shoulders. His coarse chest hair feels good as I run my hands over him.

Slowly, I lower myself to my knees, glancing up at him with my fingers on his belt, tugging slightly. "May I?" I whisper softly, and he nods, his eyes riveted to me as I methodically undo his belt and push his pants and briefs down together, freeing his thick cock. I ignore it for the moment while I help him out of his shoes and socks, and then slide his pants the rest of the way off. When he's fully naked, I sit back on my heels, admiring him. He's slim but not skinny, and a little shorter than average. Perfect size for me, since I like the feeling of being a little bigger than my partners. His dick, on the other hand, is not average sized at all. That thing would still look huge if it was attached to a giant. I lick my lips and swallow, looking up at him. His cheeks are flushed, and I can see his chest rising and falling with his rapid breaths.

I lean in slowly, nuzzling him and taking a deep breath. I stand up slowly, and then push him gently back onto the bed, following him down moments later after I've shucked off my own clothes.

He's lying on his back, his head resting on the pillows while I lie on my side next to him, resting my head on one hand while running the other over his chest, from his collarbone all the way to his dick. He's softened a little and I want to wind him right back up, but when I start to move so I can take him in my mouth, he stops me, setting a hand on my shoulder. I get concerned when I realize he's trembling.

"What's wrong?" I ask, settling back down beside him. "Am I rushing you?"

Matt shakes his head. "No, you're not doing anything wrong. I just... I'm sorry. I'm nervous."

I give him an encouraging smile. "It's okay, babe, you told me it's been a while. We'll go slow. I'm good with that."

He shakes his head, looking positively miserable. "It's not just that. I'm sorry, I should probably have told you this sooner, but I've never been with a man before."

Chapter Three

Case

"I'm sorry, what?" I ask, wondering if I heard him properly.

He lets out a huge sigh. "I've never been with another man. I'm sorry, I understand if you're not interested anymore. I should have told you before we got to this point. I'm just... Fuck, I just really want you." He laughs ruefully. "But I get it if you aren't interested in spending your night with someone who doesn't have a clue what he's doing, and apparently can't even fake it till he makes it."

My brain spins for a few moments as I process what he's telling me. *He's never been with a man before?* Jesus, do I want to be his first experience with another guy? I just wanted to have a good time, not become someone's lifelong memory. But it's clear he wants this. My protective instincts bubble up in my chest. I'll be careful not to hurt him, but not everyone he meets is going to be as concerned about that. When I look at him, he's biting down on his bottom lip so hard I'm surprised it's not bleeding. He looks so young and unsure of himself, but he's beautiful in the soft, white light spilling in through the window.

"I don't care that it's the first time you've done this with a man," I say, reaching for his hand. "But are you absolutely sure this is something you want?"

He turns to me, his eyes full of uncertainty, but there's lust in them as well. His cheeks are flushed, and his pupils are still dilated. "I've never been more sure of anything. I want you so much. I need this. Please. I need you." His voice trails off.

I reach out, extracting his abused bottom lip from between his teeth, and brush my mouth against his.

"Do you promise to tell me if I do something you don't want?" I say, staring into his eyes, trying to see if there's any doubt there.

"I promise," he whispers back. "But I want every-thing. I want you inside me. I want to be filled up and fucked. I want your hands, your mouth, your fingers on me, inside me. I want it all." He hesitates for a second before blurting out, "I want you to take charge. Tell me what to do, how to make it good. I need you to lead me."

A shudder of lust hits me like a freight train. We're essentially strangers, but he's un-inhibited enough to beg me to fuck him. I suppose since we're in our for-ties, the whole reluctant, blushing virgin routine isn't really a thing anymore, but the honesty and lack of fear in asking for what he wants is sexy as fuck.

"Okay," I whisper back to him. "I'll take care of you, Matt. Just like I promised." Desire and relief mix together on his face as he curls his hand around the back of my neck and pulls me down into him, his mouth hard and demanding on mine.

I smile into his mouth, and when I relax, he does too. I run my hands over his abs and chest slowly. Moving so I'm between his legs, I lean in and take all of him into my mouth without warning. He lets out a surprised shout, which gives way to breathless laughter as I suck hard, his cock filling and hardening immediately.

"Oh, god," he moans as I work him until he's writhing with desire.

I take my mouth off him so I can shift his hips into a better angle and grab the lube from beside him. He sucks in a breath when the cold fluid drips down between the cheeks of his ass, making me chuckle. "Sorry, baby, should have warmed it up first." I lean over to take his mouth, my hand still working between his legs, gently exploring until I reach his hole. Then I rub and circle him with one finger, gently increasing the pressure until I can feel him soften for me. Slowly, I push my finger into him, stopping at the first knuckle to let him get used to the feeling of being penetrated. It doesn't take long before he's writhing and pressing down onto my finger, craving more. I take him into my mouth again as I slide another finger inside him, and he shudders.

"Fuck," he gasps. "Feels so good."

Gently, I slide my finger in and out of him, with each thrust going just a tiny bit deeper until he's writhing and pressing down onto my hand, begging for more. Once I think he's almost at the edge, I slide a second finger into him, pausing as he gasps and stills.

"It's okay baby, give your body time to adjust." I stop moving my hand and lean forward to kiss him. By the time I've dragged my tongue down his torso, stopping to pay his nipples some attention on the way, his cock is hard again. Tentatively, I start moving my fingers in and out of him once more. Once he seems loose and relaxed enough, I slide a third into him, and he pauses again, squeezing his eyes shut and breathing through it while I rub soothing circles over his belly with my free hand. He relaxes much faster this time, and it doesn't take long before I'm spreading my fingers inside him, stretching him open slowly.

"How are you doing, are you okay?" I ask him, and he looks up at me with such raw vulnerability on his face that I almost well up. The level of trust he's placing in me right now, letting me guide him through this experience, sparks a strong urge to protect him inside me. I've never felt that way with anyone.

"I'm okay... I'm good," he whispers. "I need more, please, god. I need you inside me."

I have to close my eyes and swallow hard when I see the naked emotion on his face. I don't think anyone has ever looked at me like that. All the protective armor everyone uses to protect themselves with others is gone from his eyes. It sounds ridiculous, I know, but I feel like I can look into his eyes and I can see who he is at his very core. I know we're strangers to each other, but right now it doesn't feel that way. I don't think I've ever felt closer to another person in my life.

Taking his mouth with mine again, I slowly withdraw my fingers from his body as gently as I can. He gasps and writhes under me as I sit back on my heels to get a condom on and add a generous amount of additional lube.

"Do you want to get on all fours for me? It might be easier for you." I say softly. It's true, but if I'm totally honest, switching to that position might give me a little emotional distance from this man who's supposed to be a stranger, but doesn't feel that way at all. But as I'm quickly learning, he doesn't back away from his emotions. He blinks up at me and shakes his head.

"I need to see you. I need to see your face."

My chest gets strangely tight at his words. I feel like he needs to see me so he knows he's not alone, and no matter how uncomfortable it makes me, I'm not going to leave him alone. I'll be here for him to help him with this.

"Okay, baby. I'll do whatever you need," I say tenderly, pressing my palm to the side of his face and taking his mouth in a soft, gentle kiss. "I'm here."

MATTHEW

The world outside this room has completely ceased to exist as Case looks at me with the most gentle expression and promises he'll do what feels right for me. "This experience is nothing like what I imagined. The tenderness he's showing me, the care with which he's checking in to make sure I'm alright. This is not what I imagined sex with a stranger to be.

After getting the condom on and adding a bunch more lube to both my body and his dick, he leans forward and I feel the head of his dick at my entrance. There's a feeling of inevitability. Like this was always meant to happen just like this. I realize I'm being ridiculous, but I can't shake the feeling that even though I'm nervous, this is supposed to be happening exactly like it is.

He presses into me so slowly, I almost beg him to go faster, but I trust him. I don't know why, but I trust this stranger with whom I'm sharing one of the most important moments of my life.. My body burns as it stretches around him, but I focus on his gentle hands caressing my abdomen. Finally, he leans back and looks down at where we're joined, letting out a deep groan. One more small movement and I can feel his balls press up against me.

"That's it, I'm inside," Case whispers, lifting his gaze from where I'm impaled on him to my eyes. "Do you feel okay?"

"God yes, please move," I groan, almost sobbing as the burning inside me changes to the most intense, exquisite pleasure I've ever felt.

Doing what I ask, he starts to move, thrusting slowly at first, but as I get closer to the edge, I start pushing back on him, our bodies finding a rhythm easily.

"So good," He gasps, throwing his head back as sweat rolls down his temple. At some point, he's taken one of my legs and placed it over his shoulder. He leans down to kiss me, and that position allows him to go just a bit deeper, drawing a whimper from my throat. We both circle our hips, and I feel him so deep inside my body it turns me inside out.

"I need.. I need.." I'm a mess, not even to put into words what I need, but Case knows. Continuing to buck into me relentlessly, he works his hand between us and jerks me in time with his thrusts.

"Come for me, baby. I want to feel you come." He drags his thumb over the crown of my cock and that's it. I come harder than I ever have in my life. It feels like it lasts forever, ropes and ropes shooting out of me, covering my chest and abdomen.

He thrusts even harder and faster into me as the waves of my orgasm wane, and when I feel his cock swell and his muscles all tense as he lets out a shout as I know he's followed me over the edge.

He collapses forward onto me, smearing my release over both our bellies, both of us panting. He takes my mouth once more in a soft kiss that seems to communicate everything I need. "Are you okay?" he says, pulling his head back just enough to see my eyes.

"God, yes. So good." I say softly.

He places another gentle kiss on my lips before pulling out of me slowly. I wince as he leaves my body and I'm hit with an overwhelming feeling of emptiness. Case disappears into the bathroom for a few moments, coming back with a warm washcloth and a which he uses to clean me up gently. Then he goes into the suite kitchen, returning with a bottle of water which he hands me as he climbs back into bed. He wraps his arms around me and pulls me close. "How are you doing?" he asks softly once we're settled.

I can't seem to string together more than a word or two, since my brain has gone offline and I'm not sure when it will be back, but I manage a soft "I'm good. So good." Case squeezes me against him, and I feel safe and protected.

"You'll be sore tomorrow, but hopefully it won't be too bad." He presses his lips to my temple. "You should rest for a little while."

His soft words whispered in my ear feel like permission to let everything go, so I do. I let all the overwhelming feelings will wait until later, and as I let the soft blanket of sleep settle over me, I sigh, feeling strangely like I'm where I'm supposed to be.

Chapter Four

Matthew

I wake up with a start. It's pitch dark, and I know I'm not in my own bed. *Where the fuck am I?* I'm sweltering, and I realize there's someone in bed with me, plastered to my side. A man. I'm in bed with a man. And suddenly everything comes rushing back. I had sex with a man, and it was the most intense, hottest experience I've ever had. I close my eyes because this is all too much. I know I've done nothing wrong. Michele is moving out, and we're not getting back together. I know I've wondered a few times if maybe I might not be one hundred percent straight, but I never imagined it would lead to me waking up in another man's bed.

Fuck. Fuck. Fuck. I need to get out of here. I don't know the protocol for this situation. Do I wake him up to say goodbye? Just sneak out? Do I leave my contact info? But what if he doesn't contact me? Do I even want him to? My breathing speeds up and my chest tightens as my thoughts spiral out of control. I feel like someone's grabbed my lungs and is squeezing them. *I need to get out of here right fucking now.* If this guy wakes up while I'm in the middle of a panic attack, it's going to make things even worse, and I don't think I can handle that level of awkwardness.

My eyes have adjusted to the bit of light coming from the clock beside the bed. Case shifts around, pulling away from me so he's lying on his back with the sheets gathered around his waist and one arm resting on the pillow beside his head.

My breath catches in my throat, so I close my eyes again, trying to regulate my breathing. He moves restlessly again, this time rolling onto his side so his back is toward me. He lets out a contented sounding sigh, sinking back into what seems like a deep sleep. I give it a couple of minutes to be sure, and then I slide carefully out of bed. Using the light from my phone,

I find my clothes scattered around the floor and get dressed as fast as I can, shoving my socks into my pants pockets and slipping my bare feet into my shoes. Grabbing my suit jacket off the back of the chair, I debate leaving him a message of some kind. But what am I going to say? Thanks for the sex and have a nice life? I'm never going to see him again, so what's the point? God help me, I don't have a fucking clue. I'll just have to stay single for the rest of my life, because this is too awkward.

Shaking my head, I open the heavy hotel room door as quietly as I can, thankful there's a separate bedroom, so he's less likely to hear it. I check the hallway quickly, like I'm a teenager sneaking out after curfew, and walk out. My stomach does a strange flip as the door clicks shut behind me. My room is a couple of floors below this one, so I find the stairs at the end of the hallway and use those instead of the elevator, thankfully slipping inside without encountering anyone on my very first official walk of shame.

I'm so overwhelmed I barely know my own name right now. I'm freaked out, but I don't think it's because I slept with a man. I think it's because I slept with someone who isn't Michele. After twenty-five years together, I was worried about sleeping with anyone new. Turns out it was a much newer experience than I ever imagined. *Jesus Christ.* Clearly, I am not one hundred percent straight. That was the most incredible sexual experience I've ever had. If this is what sex with a man is like, why the hell isn't every man on the planet bisexual?

I shake my head as I take my clothes off one more time. For a moment I consider a shower, but I have a few hours before I need to get ready for the day, and for some reason I don't want to wash off Case's scent that still clings to my skin. *Weird, but I'm not even going to try and examine what that means.* I sigh as I crawl between the sheets. I guess I'll be doing a whole lot of thinking on the flight home. I've just picked up a bunch of extra baggage I'm going to have to try and unpack when I get there.

CHAPTER FIVE

CASE

Present Day

The sky over Seattle is steely gray when I head out from the little hobby farm owned by my best friend Reed and his partner, Dylan, a few days before Christmas.

Reed and I stayed up way too late last night drinking too much beer and catching up, so I got a later start than I'd planned, but my rented SUV has good snow tires. I'm excited to spend the next couple of days skiing and relaxing with a group of old college friends. This year's annual get together is at a cabin up in the

Canadian Rockies, close to some world-renowned ski hills. The place has a hot tub and every other creature comfort you can imagine. The rest of the guys arrived yesterday, but I spent one night at Reed's place in Seattle and drive up from there. I cannot wait for a couple of days of relaxation with old friends.

This little getaway is a fresh start. It's long past time to evict the specter of the man who's been living rent free in my head for over a year, preventing me from even thinking about anyone else.

'Matt From Seattle', as I now think of him, is going to be moving on out of my head beginning today. Only about a year too late.

I am not a relationship guy. I was pretty young when I learned first-hand how fragile life is, and how quickly someone you love can be taken from you, so I decided being independent is the best route for me. However, I've been caught off guard a couple of times by a couple of people who thought they were fine with a sex-only relationship, but they ended up growing attached, and things got awkward. So, I brought in a 'one-and-done' policy, and so far it's worked pretty well. I'm totally up front about it from the start. No

Repeats. No Exceptions. That is until I ran into Matt From Seattle.

He was different than anyone I've ever been with, and he's the only guy I've ever considered breaking my rule for. There was something about him I couldn't get enough of. The sex we had was unlike anything I'd ever experienced. It was incredible, like something out of a romance novel or some shit. I was so overwhelmed and wrung out that I passed out afterwards, sleeping for a couple of hours. I had thought he was feeling the same way, having a similar mind-blowing experience. It never occurred to me, in my orgasm-drunk haze, to confirm he was going to stick around for round two after we both got a little sleep. But when I woke up, he was gone. And since that night, I haven't been able to go one goddamn day without thinking about him. Not. One. Day. Reed thinks the guy's dick must be magical, and I'm inclined to agree. It is not rational for a man in his forties to be so enamored with a virtual stranger after one brief encounter. I don't even know his last name, for fuck's sake.

But this weekend marks the end of the madness. One of my old college buddies has spent the last few annual weekends trying to get me into bed, and it's become a joke among all of us. But this weekend I'm giving in. Jake is a great guy. He's a former NHL player who's still involved with the league. He's also deep in the closet, so he's ultra-choosy about who he fucks so he doesn't risk getting outed. I know he's hot; I know he's fun and I also know there isn't a chance in hell of either of us developing feelings. It's the perfect opportunity to start fresh and get my groove back.

I'm pulled out of my thoughts when I realize the light flurries that have been falling for the last couple of hours are no longer light; the snowfall coming down around me now is thick and heavy. Little white drifts are building up beside the highway and along the center dividers. Glancing at the clock, I realize that I've still got several hours of driving ahead of me. I swallow thickly when I look at the sky and realize it's no longer steely gray. It's much darker and the clouds look like they're about to burst open.

Taking a breath, I try to chase away the little seedlings of panic trying to take root. I'm not alone. There are plenty of other cars on the highway, and I'm sure the roads have been cleared. I mean, this is Canada, for god's sake. If there's one thing they probably know how to do properly, it's clear snow, right?

In the next half hour, I go from nervously reassuring myself that I'll be fine, to absolutely white-knuckling it. Traffic has slowed to barely a crawl, and I can hardly see the taillights of the vehicle in front of me.

Shit, shit, shit. What am I going to do? I have a fear of being in a situation where I can't contact anyone or call for help. When we were young, Reed and I were in a serious car accident, and I still bear some trauma from the experience. We were stuck in our overturned car at the bottom of a ditch for what felt like hours, and I'll never forget the feeling of knowing, just knowing, I was going to die. In reality, we'd been rescued pretty quickly, even though it did not feel that way to either of us.

Sitting in the car, snow falling so hard, the only thing I can see is a wall of white. The tendrils of panic creep up my spine and curl their way into my chest. They wrap around my lungs, making it hard to take a deep breath. I know how to ward off a panic attack. It's been a long time since I've had one, but my training comes back to me like riding a bike. I continue breathing as deeply as I can, and try to count five things I can see, hear, smell, and touch. Reconnecting with my senses helps me stave off the panic, and within a few minutes I can feel my heart rate slow down.

After we've been completely stopped for a while, I see the red and blue lights of a police car moving slowly toward me. It pauses briefly every few minutes and then approaches again. Thank god, at least they're giving us information. Hopefully, they'll have good news, and we won't be stuck here long.

As they approach my car, I roll down the window for the bundled-up cop walking alongside the cruiser, holding one of those giant flashlights.

"Evening, Officer. Please tell me you've got some good news about the road?" I say, fighting to keep the nerves out of my voice.

The guy laughs. "Sorry, son. I wish I had better news for you, but we have to shut it down. We've already had two serious accidents, and the weather's gonna get a whole lot worse over the next few hours."

"Well, crap," I say with a grimace. "What are you all suggesting people do?"

He offers me a sympathetic smile. "Well, you've got two options: you can turn around and head back toward the coast, or you can stick it out here for the night and hope they can open the road in the morning. If you want my personal opinion, though, I think that's pretty unlikely. This storm feels like a big one."

"Aaargh," I say eloquently, leaning my head against the steering wheel. My visions of a relaxing couple of days with friends fading away and being replaced by unpleasant images of a long drive back to the coast in terrible conditions.

"Honestly, son, my recommendation is to turn back. My guess is the road's gonna be closed for a few days." He smiles kindly. "I wish I had better news for you."

I smile ruefully, thanking him as he heads toward the next car.

Dammit. What the fuck do I do now?

I should probably take the cop's advice and start heading back, but before beginning my hellish drive, I decide to indulge myself in a little pity-party. I grab the phone to call Reed so I can bitch and complain at him for a bit, and also let him know I'll be back at his place sooner than planned.

After updating him on my current predicament though, instead of the expected laughter, I get a tense-sounding silence.

"Reed, you know I'm not pissed at you, right?" I ask. "I was just fucking around. It's totally my fault I left late. I just felt like whining and thought it would be funny to blame you."

"Yeah, yeah, I know," he says. "But Dylan and I've been checking the news. The weather office just issued some kind of crazy weather warning I've never seen before. They're telling people to get inside and batten down the hatches. This storm is huge, and it's going to hammer the hell out of the whole Pacific Northwest for the next two or three days. Hurricane-force winds are going to be felt way farther inland than ever before. Road conditions are horrible already and they're getting worse fast. I'm worried about you being out there at all."

"Well, shit." I lean my head against the steering wheel again in frustration. "That's not exactly what I was hoping to hear."

CHAPTER SIX

MATTHEW

I'm on the road Monday morning, venti caramel latte in hand, my SUV packed to the gills with everything I could need for a few days away. At first, I was reluctant to accept the offer of the luxury mountain cabin owned by my friend and second in command at my company, Hunter Davies, but as I head out bright and early, I have to admit I'm looking forward to it.

It's been a long year, but now that my divorce from Michele is finally complete, Hunter convinced me to 'honor my experience' by taking a few days to reset. Hunter's a bit more hipster than me, but I have to admit, after the last few years of 'go go go', I'm ready to take my brain out and simply exist for a little while. The cabin is on the Canadian side of the border, nestled in the Rocky Mountains. Apparently there are no neighbors within sight, so it's completely private (a feature that Hunter's new husband, Penn, made sure to tell me about.) He also made sure to let me know how amazing it is to hang out in the hot-tub, bathing suit optional, naturally, while the snow falls around you. According to Penn it's practically a life-changing experience. Being a hermit for the next few days sounds remarkably good.

Around lunchtime, I pull into a gas station to fill up and grab some peanut butter cups because even though I'm not religious, I'm pretty sure it's against one of the commandments to take a road trip without road snacks. The clerk smiles as he's placing my haul into a bag. "I hope you've got good snow tires. It's supposed to turn real nasty out there," he says as I hand him my credit card.

"Oh, is that right?" I ask.

He nods. "They've been talking about it for the last couple of days. Massive storm coming. They say it's gonna hit hard all the way down into the states for the whole week. You need to drive real careful and make sure your tires are good, eh?"

"Good thing I brought enough supplies to last me a month, then," I laugh.

"With the way this storm is shaping up, you might need it." He grins at me. "You drive safe now," he calls as I walk out the door and I reply with a wave of thanks.

A couple of hours later, my GPS leads me up a winding mountain road that feels more like logging track than the route to an enclave of luxurious mountain homes. But after a few minutes, I come around a sharp bend to find one of the most beautiful views I've ever seen.

"Whoa," I say out loud. Hunter wasn't kidding when he said the place was like a resort. The main house is an A-frame style building, the yellow color of the enormous cedar logs contrasting beautifully with the green metal roof. It definitely looks more like a fabulous chalet than a little mountain cabin.

Grabbing one of my bags, I head inside, and it's just as breathtaking as the outside. In the main living area, the ceiling soars up two stories, with a chandelier hanging from the wood paneled ceiling and a huge stone fireplace at the far end. Floor-to-ceiling windows face out onto the Rockies, their craggy, jagged peaks poking up into the canvas of gray sky.

The kitchen looks like it's fit for a fit for a five-star chef, with stunning marble countertops and shining stainless steel appliances. There's a massive island surrounded by several chocolate-brown leather barstools for extra eating space.

The primary bedroom suite on the other side of the cabin boasts more huge windows looking out across the large yard down to the river and the steep mountains beyond.

"Not too shabby," I mutter, admiring the view from the bedroom. The shadows have already started to lengthen, and a few snowflakes are fluttering down from the gray sky, so I head back outside to haul in the rest of my supplies. I'm eager to get on with the business of relaxing.

After I get everything inside, I decide to make myself spaghetti for dinner. I have my Sicilian Nonna's old family recipe that always reminds me of my mother and is legitimately good enough to make a grown man cry. I won't have time to let it sit and simmer all day like it's supposed to, so maybe it won't move me to tears, but it will be good anyway.

Chapter Seven

Case

Reed's reaction to my being stuck out here in the wilderness in the middle of *Snowmageddon* isn't exactly reassuring, but there isn't much I can do about it. I'll make it out of here somehow.

"Fucking hell. Well, I guess I'd better get moving. Wish me luck." I sigh, pinching the bridge of my nose.

"Wait a second, I have an idea. Can you drop a pin and show me exactly where you are?" Reed asks. I do and then hear him tapping away on his phone. A minute later, he adds me to a group text thread with his friend Penn Thompson.

> Penn: Case! OMG! I can't believe you're stuck on that damn dan-

gerous road. You need to go to our cabin right now! Hunter and I are out of town, so it's empty. It's totally decked out. You'll love it. I'm sending directions and instructions for how to get in.

Me: Hey Penn. Sounds amazing. I'll take you up on that offer. This weather is shit.

Reed: Seriously, Case the place is fantastic. It's like a private resort.

Penn: It really is great. We usually rent it out, but Hunter had it blocked off in case we decided to use it for the holidays so it's all yours. Now go! Get off that highway!

Me: Thank you so much Penn. And thank Hunter too, I really appreciate this.

Penn: Anytime, Case. Seriously. Now, turn your ass around. The roads up to the cabin should be cleared by a private contractor,

> *but drive carefully Cell service is spotty but try to text when you get there.*

> *Me: I owe you guys huge for this. Thank you again.*

Breathing a sigh of relief, I turn the car around and crawl back down the steep mountain highway. Penn and his husband Hunter are friends of Reed and Dylan's. They met when Hunter's construction company built the shelter for LGBTQ teenagers that Penn runs, and the two couples got to be close friends. His shelter has even provided some data for the study my research group is working on. I can't even put into words how relieved I am that I don't have to spend three or four more hours driving in this shitty weather.

It takes over an hour to inch my way back down the highway to the exit, and then back up the steep mountain road to their cabin. Just when I'm starting to wonder if I screwed up the directions, I see lights in the distance. *Thank fuck.*

I ease the car into the long drive leading toward the house. The snow is coming down so hard I can barely see, but it looks like the cabin is an A-frame style with huge picture windows. Warm light is spills out, trying its best to illuminate the night, but the snow is falling so fast, that's nearly impossible. Opening the door of the SUV, I suddenly realize there's another car parked in the driveway, almost totally buried in snow.

Shit. Maybe someone rented it after all, and Penn forgot? I think about texting him to check, but the temperature feels like it's dropped about fifty degrees in the last hour. With the wind howling like a freight train, the snow feels like a thousand tiny needles stabbing my face. *Fuck this shit.* I'm not staying out here. Whoever's inside will just need to let me in, and we'll figure it out. It's unlikely Penn and Hunter rented their house to an axe murderer, so I'm probably safe.

I grab my big backpack and trudge up the few steps to the door. Taking a deep breath, I ring the bell and wait to meet the mystery person who's about to get a surprise roommate for the night.

Chapter Eight

Matthew

There's something comforting about being safe and warm in a mountain hideaway like this while the world outside gets gradually covered with a fluffy white blanket. My grandmother's spaghetti sauce is simmering away on the gas cooktop while I enjoy a glass of the beautiful red wine I brought.

I've only been here a few hours, and I can feel the tension draining out of me already. It will be good to have my biggest daily decision be what to make myself for dinner. Maybe it's partly the setting, and partly the fact that all the questions about my marriage are finally resolved, but I'm feeling more comfortable and settled right now than I have in a year.

I think back to the night last fall I spent with Case, and the familiar twinge of regret squeezes my chest. God, I wish I'd left him my number. Or gotten his. Or even that I'd stayed until he'd woken up so I could tell him how amazingly life changing that night was. Not that I realized it at the time.

After I made my escape that night, and after getting over my panic and shock at what went down. I realized there was a whole lot I didn't know about myself. The biggest and most obvious, of course, being that I'm not as straight as I'd always believed. In one of my best decisions yet, I found a good therapist and spent many, *many* hours unpacking my baggage from the divorce, my guilt over putting work ahead of my family so often, and my late-in-life discovery that I'm attracted to men. Derek, my therapist, helped me realize I'm not crazy or completely lacking in self-awareness. Like a lot of people, I've spent my whole life doing exactly what was expected of me, so it's not a complete surprise that I never imagined anything different.

Eventually, I landed on bisexual as a label that seems to fit best, although since that night with Case I've barely noticed women at all. The truth is, I haven't been able to stop thinking about him. Whenever my brain is idle, it's that night I think of. Replaying it has lulled me back to sleep after a satisfying orgasm more times than I can even count.

I've even been on a few dates with men, but there's been no one I wanted to sleep with since Case—man or woman. No one has sparked the same crazy desire he did. But a new year is coming. My divorce is finalized, I've settled into a reasonably healthy new dynamic with Michele and the kids, and I feel like things are looking up. I'm so glad Hunter convinced me to use the cabin this week. It helps to do something completely different than normal, so it's not as obvious this will be the first Christmas I've ever spent without my family.

As I'm cleaning up the last of the prep work from the sauce, I wonder idly if there are any cabins for sale around here. Or maybe I should build my own. It would be amazing to have a place I could get away to whenever I want.

Of course, it's so rare that I take both weekend days off, I'd probably never use it. But then a crazy thought jumps into my head. What if I looked into reducing the time I spend at work? I could learn something new, develop a hobby, or learn a language or something. I've already earned more money than I could ever spend, and after a lifetime of chasing financial success, maybe I should think about stepping back.

"Pffft." I make a frustrated noise as I finish wiping down the counter. It's an interesting thought, but I'm not sure I'd function properly without coming into the office every day. After all, I've spent far more time there than I have at my home. I shake my head. I'll probably just keep on doing what I've been doing for decades. I can't imagine my life any other way. But I make a note to talk to Derek about it at our next appointment.

After throwing another log on the fire, I snuggle into one of the comfortable recliners and watch the snow fall through the big picture window while enjoying another glass of wine. I have a strange feeling I'm exactly where I should be, which is weird. Maybe the fresh mountain air is already getting to me.

Chuckling to myself, I grab the remote. I'm about to start channel surfing when I'm shocked by the sound of knocking at the door, followed by the chime of the doorbell.

What in the hell? It must be some kind of emergency. Why else would anyone be out in this storm? I hurry to the door and wrench it open, only to nearly lose my balance and fall flat on my face.

Standing on the doorstep of this cabin in the middle of nowhere, looking like a snowman with a bright red nose and frosted eyelashes, is the man I spent the hottest night of my life with a year ago. Case. Yes, That Case. The guy I never dreamed I'd see again. That Case is standing at the door.

His eyes get big and round as recognition crosses his face.

"What the fuck?" we say at the same time.

CASE

It only takes a moment for the door to be wrenched open after I knock. I'm sure whoever's inside is wondering who the fuck is out gallivanting around in the middle of the *Snowpocalypse.* When I realize it's Matt, the guy I've spent the last year thinking about and to whom I compare every date I go on, I do a literal double take.

"What the fuck?" we say at the same time. He looks as shocked as I feel, and there's an awkward moment of silence while we both stand there speechless, our faces wearing the same stunned expression and our mouths opening and closing silently like a couple of fish gasping for air.

"Umm.. well, um hello... What, uh, what are you doing here?" he asks awkwardly. It's snowing so hard, and the wind is so strong it's blowing through the doorway and forming a tiny little snowdrift in one of the corners of the foyer.

"Uh, I'm happy to explain, but could I come in?" I ask.

"Oh, shit, of course, I'm sorry," he jumps out of the way, opening the door wider so I can step inside. The wind is so strong he has to use his body weight to close the door against the force of it. But as soon as it's shut, all traces of the storm disappear. There isn't even a draft sneaking in through the cracks. It's like the entire world outside ceases to exist.

"Here, let me take your coat. Come in." He smiles, but I just step inside, not making any move to take off my coat or boots. I feel like I've stepped into the *Twilight Zone* or some shit. How is this person, this complete stranger from a year ago who lives hundreds of miles away, how is this person is standing in front of me right now?

"Yeah. I, ah, I'm kind of confused.. How.. Why are you in my friends' cabin in the middle of the Canadian Rocky Mountains?" I ask, trying not to be rude, but my head is spinning.

He smiles. "I could ask you the same thing. But I'll go first. This place is owned by someone I work with, Hunter Davies. He and his husband are away for the holidays and Hunter offered me the cabin for this week. I got here this afternoon. Your turn."

"Right. Right. That makes sense." I mutter. I know Hunter works for some video game company; he's apparently had a meteoric rise over the last few years. But Reed and Dylan know Penn better than Hunter, so that's about all I know.

"Penn and Hunter are friends of my best friend, Reed Morrow. I was on my way to spend a few days skiing at a place a couple of hours further up the highway, but the weather closed the road. I called Reed, and when he found out where I was he contacted Penn who told me I should come here until the weather clears."

"Oh.. right. That makes sense I guess." Matt nods his head slowly. "Well, ah, come on in. I'll show you around and you can choose a bedroom. I mean – I assume you'll stay? The place is huge, more than enough space for both of us."

"Um. Yeah, I guess. I don't really like the thought of fighting this weather back down to the coast, and they say the storm is getting worse." I say, still not quite believing what's happening.

As Matt leads me through the huge living room with a stunning two-story high stone fireplace taking up one full wall, a cell phone chimes, and he grabs it off a side table. Looking at the screen he chuckles, and when he looks up at me his eyes are twinkling. A jolt of electricity runs from my balls up my spine when his eyes meet mine.

"Cell service is a little sketchy, I guess, because it looks like this text was sent an hour ago, but the notification just came now. It's Hunter. He was at the gym working out when your friend talked to Penn. Penn didn't realize Hunter offered the place to me this week, so he didn't have a chance to warn me you'd be coming." He grins at me again and damn, my knees go weak. "But he says here you're a 'great guy and definitely not a serial killer'."

I let out a snort of laughter. "I hope you're reassured."

"Definitely."

He hasn't changed much, if at all, from a year ago. I still have trouble looking away from him. He has these huge brown eyes, almost too big for his face, but somehow it works on him. He's shorter than me, and I remember vividly how perfectly his body lined up with mine, and how good the rough hair on his chest and legs felt against my skin.

With the mystery of how we ended up here together solved, we stand in the living room and stare at each other for a moment. I wonder if he's having the same erotic flashbacks I am. It's like my body recognizes who I'm talking to, and against my wishes, my cock has started to fill.

After he's shown me around, I pick one of the spacious guest rooms and after taking a few minutes to clean up a little, I head back to the kitchen where I smell something absolutely delicious.

"Can I get you a glass of wine?" Matt asks. "There's spaghetti for dinner if you're interested. My Sicilian grandmother's sauce."

"Whoa, I'm not about to turn down a Sicilian grandma's spaghetti sauce," I grin.

"Good, because it's a life changing experience. I can't make it as well as she did, but I swear to you it has moved grown men to tears in the past. It's that good."

I laugh. "You sold me. And I'll take a glass of wine. It appears I'm not going to be going anywhere tonight, that's for sure." I nod at the window where the snow is coming down so fast it's as if the window looks out on a blank, white wall.

Matt walks over to the bottle of cabernet sauvignon sitting on the counter.

After handing me a glass, he bites his lip, betraying his nervousness, and my shoulders unclench from relief. At least I'm not the only one who feels weird about this.

"So, um, this situation feels a little strange. I'm not really sure how to..." he lets his words trail off.

"I hear you," I say. "Weird twist of fate, right? Both of us ending up trapped here?"

"Um, yeah. For sure. What are the chances?" He shakes his head, and then turns to the stove and lifts the lid off the big pot containing the sauce. It smells like heaven, and my stomach lets out a huge growl.

"Whoa, you are hungry! We'd better get this plated before your stomach starts trying to eat your other internal organs!" He smirks at me and grabs a couple of plates, dishing out two generous servings of spaghetti.

He opens the oven and pulls out a basket of garlic bread that's been keeping warm, and my mouth waters, salivating like Pavlov's dog. Yeah, I'm hungry.

He nods at the basket of garlic bread on the counter as he brings the plates of spaghetti over to the big farmhouse table on one side of the kitchen, so I grab it and we take our seats. Taking a bite, I can't hold back a moan.

"*Holy shit on a shingle.* I think I just had an out of body experience." I gasp because the sauce really is that good.

He responds with the most adorable smile, a hint of pink staining his cheeks. "Thanks. I think Nonna would be satisfied with that reaction.

Chapter Nine

Matthew

Case's moan when he tastes Nonna's sauce is nearly enough to make me come in my pants, and I have to shift in my chair to my dick doesn't get completely squished. I don't think my brain has quite accepted what's happening here. I keep expecting to wake up. Like this is some kind of weird, ultra-vivid dream. Twelve hours ago, I was packing up my car to spend a few days alone at a remote cabin, and now I'm sitting here in what basically amounts to a palace in the mountains with the man who rocked my world so thoroughly that I've been unable to stop thinking about him for a year.

After he recovers from the first bites of spaghetti, we eat in comfortable silence. Clearly Case really was starving, because he scarfs down his first plate, and then hops up eagerly to get another helping.

"God, this is fantastic, thank you again," he says when he's slowed down enough to breathe.

"You must have been a nightmare to keep fed when you were a teenager," I remark with a grin, letting my eyes trail over his tall, solid body. He's definitely over six feet, and I know from our one night together that he's in great shape. I have to close my eyes for a second when my brain flashes back to the feeling of his hot, sweaty skin sliding against my own. *And there we go.* Between his moan when he tasted the sauce, and my body's determination to embarrass the shit out of me, I'm rock hard.

Case chuckles as he takes another bite. "Yeah, between me and my four brothers, I think my mom pretty much lived at the grocery store when we were growing up."

"Whoa, you have four brothers?"

"Plus one sister," he says with a smirk. "But to be fair, the last two were twins, so my parents weren't actually expecting to have that many kids. Although my mom likes to say that once you get to three kids, adding a few more makes no difference, because once the parents are outnumbered, all bets are off. My dad would joke about parents of more than two kids having to play zone defense instead of man-to-man coverage, so three kids or five didn't change anything."

I smile, "I had three, and I have to say I don't think adding any more would have been a good idea. Michele always had her hands full."

He smiles. "How about you?" he asks. "Any siblings you grew up causing trouble with?"

I shake my head. "Nope, only child. My house was probably a lot less chaotic than yours. I used to wonder what it would be like to have a brother or sister though. But I probably wouldn't have liked sharing my mom's attention."

Case grabs the wine bottle, splitting the last of it between our glasses.

"Aah, so you were a mama's boy growing up, huh?" His eyes twinkle as he teases me.

I laugh. "You could say that, I guess. My dad worked a lot of hours, so my mom and I spent a lot of time together when I was young." I smile, those fuzzy memories being some of my favorites.

"Nice. Are you still close with her?" he asks, taking a sip of wine.

I clear my throat. "I think I would be, but she passed away when I was a teenager. My dad raised me after that."

Case's eyes go wide. "I'm so sorry. I can't imagine losing my mom so young." He reaches out and places his big hand over mine where it's resting on the table.

"It's okay. It was a long time ago. Losing her at a young age meant she missed my 'rebellious asshole stage', so all my memories of her are good. We never fought." I smile.

There's a slightly awkward pause in our conversation before I clear my throat and get up to clear the dishes away. Case hops up to help, and it doesn't take long to get the kitchen cleaned up.

Working together seems to have eased the awkward tension, and it's still early evening. "Another bottle?" I suggest. "They've got Netflix, so we could watch a movie."

Case hesitates, glancing at his watch like he needs to run off somewhere, but then he looks out the window and lets out a laugh. The snow is still coming down heavily and the wind continues to buffet the house so hard the windows occasionally shake from the force of it. "Well, it doesn't look like I'm going anywhere for a while, so let's go for it!"

Chapter Ten

Case

Matt opens a second bottle of red wine, and we head into the living room, where I settle into a comfy, oversized chair in front of the big stone fireplace. Matt throws another log onto the fire before getting himself settled in the cozy chair across from mine.

I feel bad about accidentally bringing up Matt's mom. It sounds like he's not close to his father, and he seemed a little lonely. But I'm no stranger to the grieving someone you love. It's been so long since Danny's death the grief isn't as intense anymore, but it's wound that will never heal completely. Every so often something happens that rips off the scab, and it hurts almost as much as it did at first. Fortunately for me, as the years have gone on, that's happened less often, but I know it's always there.

"Can I ask you a question?" I say, out of the blue, and he smiles at me over the rim of his glass.

"Go for it."

"I don't want you to take this the wrong way, but I just was wondering what made you sneak out that night in Chicago?"

Matt splutters and coughs in shock.

I feel like an idiot. "You know what, I'm sorry, I don't know why I asked," I babble. "You were dealing with a lot that night, and it's my fault for accidentally falling asleep on you. I'm so sorry about that, by the way. You didn't do anything wrong." I waggle my eyebrows and decide to try joking with him for distraction. "I was just so disappointed when I woke up. I'd been looking forward to another round." Matt doesn't crack a smile. Instead, he looks thoroughly embarrassed, which makes me feel even worse.

"No, I'm the one who's sorry. I wanted to say something about it. I just didn't know how to bring it up." He clears his throat.

He takes a deep breath and studies the contents of his wineglass. "I snuck out because I was on the verge of a full-fledged panic attack, and I didn't want you to see me lose it."

"Shit, Matt, I'm sorry. I was so upset with myself when I realized I'd fallen asleep on you. You probably needed someone to talk to, and I just passed out."

He shakes his head. "No, no way. Do not apologize. The whole experience with you was... incredible. I never knew I could-," he swallows. When he takes a sip from his wineglass his hand trembles slightly, and my chest gets tight.

Taking a deep breath, he finally meets my eyes. "I was so lost that night. I had no idea what my life was going to look like, I just knew it wasn't going to be anything like I had planned. But you.. you made me feel so fucking good, Case. You gave me exactly what I needed; I just didn't know how to process the emotions. I couldn't deal with the grief over the divorce, together with the euphoria I felt after we.. were together. It was too much, and I needed to leave before you saw me lose it." He stops and clears his throat. "This might sound ridiculous, but that night changed my life. For the better. I will always be grateful to you for that night. No matter what."

"What do you mean, it changed your life?"

"I was struggling with who I was, even before you and I met. But I don't think I had even recognized what I was struggling with. That night forced me to face some things about myself. In one of my smarter moves, I went into therapy shortly after that, and I've spent the last year working out a lot of shit. Stuff I should have worked out a long time ago."

I lean forward, placing my wine glass carefully on the coffee table and then turning my full attention to Matt. "Really?"

He nods. "Really. I wished so often that I'd stayed, or woken you up, or left my contact info. But in the end it was better I didn't. I don't think I would have been able to deal with all my issues if I we were in contact."

"Oh. Um. Wow." I look away and drag a hand through my hair before getting up and taking the few steps over to the fireplace, staring into the flames. Is he saying he's been thinking about me for the last year, the same way I've been thinking about him? I swallow, hoping my voice doesn't shake when I speak.

"So. Your therapy. What have you learned?"

He laughs. "God, I'd need hours to tell you all the shit I've uncovered. I'll say this: money may not be able to buy you happiness or love, but it can buy you a really great therapist, which is pretty much as good as those other two things."

I chuckle. "Well, on behalf of psychologists everywhere, thank you for that."

"You're welcome. But in all honesty Case, and I know this sounds ridiculous, but that night changed my life. It was incredible."

I can't help it, a snort of laughter escapes me, the overwrought seriousness of the moment getting to me, and I turn to face him. "Wow, I have to say, I've received some compliments in my life, but I'm not sure I've ever been told my dick is life-changing."

Matt hesitates for a moment, then lets out a loud bark of laughter, grabs a throw pillow from the couch beside him, and tosses it at my head.

"Asshole," he grins, and a warm, fuzzy feeling settles over me like a blanket. That smile of his is what's life changing. Forget about my dick. When he smiles like no one's watching, it's like the sun breaking through the clouds. Matt seems like someone who's always on guard, monitoring his own reactions to everything, making sure he's behaving appropriately. Every so often, the guard comes down and I get a glimpse of someone else. Someone a lot less concerned with what anyone else thinks. That's the guy I met last year, the one I brought back to my hotel room and had the most intense experience of my life with.

He gets off the couch and comes to stand beside me in front of the fireplace.

"I know it sounds stupid and overly dramatic, but it's true," he says so quietly I can barely hear him over the crackling of the fireplace. "I had never.. I didn't.." He stops himself and shakes his head. "I'd never experienced that kind of intensity, that level of passion, of... connection. I loved Michele, but we never had anything like that." He shakes his head and blows out a long breath. "I'm probably a fool for telling you this, but I haven't been able to stop thinking about that night – about you – for a year."

It's like all the oxygen drains out of the room, and I turn to face him. His eyes are wide, like he's surprised at what just came out of his mouth.

"You... You've been thinking about me for the past year?" My voice is low and rough.

He nods, his chest rising and falling quickly as his breathing shallows and color fills his cheeks. "I haven't been able to get you out of my head. I think about you all the time. I replay that night over and over again."

My heart skips a beat. Literally skips a beat like I'm about to have a goddamn heart attack. But he's been thinking about me the same way I've been thinking about him. Suddenly, I feel like my belly is on fire; the flames licking up my body from my balls all the way up to my chest and down to my toes.

I step closer to him so we're standing chest to chest.

"I've thought about you too. I can't get that night out of my head." I say, my own breathing heavy.

I don't know who moves first, but our mouths crash together and in that moment I know there's no turning back. My strict 'one and done' rule is getting tossed out the window and I can't fucking wait.

I grab his hips and haul him in close to me as he wraps his arms tightly around my neck. We stand just like that and kiss for a long time, and it nearly sends me over the moon. Finally I have to pull back for air, and I press my forehead to his, both of us panting. He runs the palm of his hand over my chest like he can't touch enough of me. "I have an idea," I say softly, and he looks at me with curiosity, still pressed up against me.

"What are you thinking?" He asks. "Because if it's the same as what I'm thinking, we should maybe take this to the bedroom... or at least over to the couch.."

I laugh and bend down to nibble on the side of his neck. "You mentioned there's a hot tub here? We should make use of it before we lose power. What do you think?"

Matt pulls his head back, an evil grin on his face, and I fucking love it. Even though he hasn't been with anyone else since our encounter over a year ago, his confidence has increased by leaps and bounds, and it's sexier than I would have ever imagined. I fucking love it.

"I think I'll race you out there."

Chapter Eleven

Matthew

The hot tub is in a separate room attached to the house, but it almost feels like a separate building. Three of the walls are glass, but it's the fancy stuff that you can turn dark if you don't want anyone to see in. When I look closer, I realize the glass panels are all moveable, so you could open all the walls and you'd be unsheltered except for the one side closest to the main house. But this setup is perfect for right now, because the wind is howling, and I'm not sure it would be too pleasant if we were exposed to all the elements. The room also has outdoor heaters mounted around the edges of the ceiling, making it perfect for nights like this. I find the switch to turn them on, and then take the cover off the hot tub, breathing in the billowing steam that rises as soon as the icy cold air hits the hot water.

My cock has been hard as steel since Case touched me. Once he shows up in swim trunks, I'm going to lose any semblance of control, so I should probably get into the water, so it's not as obvious. I'll consider it a win if I can stop myself from jumping him the moment he gets outside. Grabbing my wine glass and setting it on the side, I slide quickly out of the fuzzy white robe I found in the bedroom, and stick my freezing feet in, hissing as the hot water makes contact.

I slide the rest of my body in until the water is up to my neck, and I'm not gonna lie. It's glorious. I'm getting comfortable with one jet hitting my lower back at exactly the right spot, when the sliding glass door opens and Case steps outside, his face breaking into a pleased smile when he sees me.

"How is it?" he asks, tossing his robe on the chair beside mine and sliding out of the cozy slippers. He tiptoes quickly over to the side of the tub and lets out the same hiss as I did when the hot water hits his cold skin.

"Fuuuck that's good..." He closes his eyes and throws his head back as the rest of his body disappears under the water.

We're both quiet for a few minutes, letting the hot water soothe us. There's something about an outdoor hot tub when it's snowing that's almost magic.

Case is the first one to break the silence. "Maybe we'll get lucky, and the power won't go out. I think I could stay in here for a week." He shifts to allow the jet behind him to hit a different part of his lower back, although I think I saw a little extra adjustment as he shifted his hips, which causes me to bite back a smile.

As soon as those words are out of his mouth, the electric heaters flicker briefly, making us both chuckle.

"We should probably enjoy it while we can." I say, extending my legs under the water and enjoying the way my muscles feel as they stretch out in the warmth.

Case's eyes are still closed, his head tipped back, mouth open slightly. The position of his head exposes his neck, and goddammit if I don't want to float over to him and suck it until I leave a mark. *Jesus fuck*. I've never wanted to claim another person, but I have this weird, primal desire to mark Case so the entire world knows who he belongs to.

He opens his eyes slowly and hits me with a look that feels like a physical caress. He drags his gaze over my face, lingering on my mouth for a few moments before sliding lower, trying to make out the blurry lines of my body underneath the water.

"You're too far away over there," he grins lazily. "You should come closer to me."

He's looking at me with such intensity there's a part of me that wants to look away, afraid of what he might see. He licks his lips slowly, and my breath hitches as he reaches for me. Carefully, he takes my drink out of my hand, placing it carefully on the tub surround. Then, with both hands, he takes my wrists and pulls me slowly through the water toward him. As he settles back into the seat, he brings me closer, so I'm straddling his lap, with my hands on his shoulders. I'm hard as a rock, my dick straining against the thin material of my swim trunks. I resist the overwhelming urge to grind down on him, even as I can feel his hard cock straining against his shorts, and I can't hide the shiver that runs through me.

"Is this okay?" he asks softly. His eyes haven't left mine.

I nod, almost unable to form words, but somehow I manage to squeak out a "yes" before he stretches up to kiss me, our mouths meeting in a scorching tangle of teeth and lips and tongue. My temperature seems to rise another hundred degrees as he puts his hands on my hips and pulls me down at the same time as he presses up against me so our erections are pressed together, just like I've been craving.

I move my hands to either side of his face, sliding my tongue into his mouth, roughly taking possession. His groan and the shudder that passes through his body only spur me on, and I grind my cock down into his with an almost frantic need.

"Fuck, Case.. I've been thinking about this for a year." My voice is hoarse.

"Me too," he gasps against my mouth.

Without taking his lips off mine, he lifts my hips and slides his hands under the waistband of my shorts, pushing them down my legs so I can kick them off. Feeling the water around my dick with no fabric covering it makes me gasp again. Case lifts his hips, still holding me away from him so I can yank his shorts down far enough so he can kick them off. I don't waste any time, wrapping my hand around his cock greedily and squeezing before I settle back onto his lap. As soon as I'm back in position, I release him and instead press into him again, desperately seeking friction to find some relief. Our cocks push and grind against each other, the heads catching occasionally as they slide through the water.

Case's cheeks are flushed, beads of sweat forming on his forehead. His eyes are wild when he opens them to look at me, almost out of control, and that gives me a burst of confidence.

"I want to suck you," I gasp, leaning forward to suck on his neck again. "Fuck, I want to feel you in my mouth. Can I? Please?"

"Ohh fuck..." he groans. "Are you sure? We didn't do that last time.."

"Fuck yes, I'm sure. I've been dreaming about it for a year." I say indignantly.

He chuckles. "Far be it from me to deny a man the chance to live his dream," he smirks and braces his hands against the side to pull himself out of the water to perch on the edge. Before I can get into position, he reaches over to the small remote control sitting on the deck and presses a button which closes the one sliding glass door that's open, protecting us from the wind on all four sides, and when he presses a couple more buttons, the roof of the room slides open like a stadium, so it's open to the sky.

"Holy shit, that's incredible," I gasp, looking up through the open roof. Since we're literally in the middle of a blizzard, there are no stars visible, but the snow is falling through the opening in the roof, giving us tiny little zings when the cold flakes hit our hot, wet skin. We can hear the wind, but we're sheltered from most of it and the heaters do the rest of the work to keep the surrounding air warm enough that we don't freeze. Whoever designed this place thought of everything.

A moment later, my gaze returns to Case's hard cock. I swallow thickly, and he looks at me with concern. "Are you okay? You don't have to-"

"I told you; I want to! Stop trying to make decisions for me," I snark, and then gasp, not sure where the bratty outburst came from, but when I look at him, his eyes have darkened even further, making him look even more turned on. He grabs the base of his cock and squeezes, closing his eyes as he works on slowing his breathing.

"Fuck, feeling a little bratty, are we?" he whispers. You'd better behave, Mister Cartwright. I'd hate to have to turn you over my knee."

My breath catches and I have to grab my own dick so I don't spontaneously come in the water. *Jesus H. Christ on a piece of toast. Do I want to be spanked?* My cock jerks at the thought. *Fuck, maybe I do. That's new.* We stare at each other for a moment. I don't know what to say, but he takes charge effortlessly.

"That sounds hot as fuck, but let's save it for another time," he whispers, and I nod.

He leans back on one elbow, a devious grin on his face, and gives his shaft a long, slow stroke, "Well, Mister 'I make my own decisions', I'm ready whenever you are." He gives me a saucy wink, as if to reassure me that none of this has to be a huge deal. We're just two people having fun. It doesn't have to turn into a giant, anxiety-inducing event.

His cock is still wet, a few drops of water clinging to the shaft and his neatly trimmed pubes. A pearl of shiny precum glistens at the tip, and without thinking about it, I dart my tongue out and lick it off, letting out a groan of pleasure as I taste him. Flattening my tongue, I start at the base and lick a long, slow strip up the bottom, finishing with a swirl of my tongue around the crown. He lets out a moan that goes right to my balls, and I feel a surge of power. He's experiencing this pleasure because of me. With one hand, I grab his base, and without breaking eye contact, wrap my lips around him, drawing a deep groan from his throat.

I hold him in my mouth for a moment, getting used to what it feels like. The weight of him on my tongue feels incredible. He's big enough that I have to open my mouth wide to fit him inside, and I know my jaw is probably going to ache, but it will be worth it.

His breathing is shaky, and I can tell he's holding back from thrusting into me. I suck him slowly, appreciating how he's hard as steel, but he's covered in skin that's soft as velvet. I alternate between hard and gentle suction, humming with pleasure, moving slowly. My fingers dig into his strong thighs and my confidence grows with each soft moan he gives me.

"Fuck yes, oh god that's so good," he whispers.

I shove aside all my insecurities and focus on giving him pleasure, sucking him as deep into my throat as I can without triggering my gag reflex.

"Oh fuuuck, Matt. Oh god yes." He gasps, closing his eyes, and burying one hand in my hair, gripping it just tightly enough that I can feel it sting. I let out a porn-worthy groan of my own, and I can't help thrusting my hips in the water, in desperate search of relief for my aching, throbbing cock. I move a certain way and one jet hits me just right, causing me to gasp around Case's dick. His balls are pulled tight against his body, and I feel him grow bigger in my mouth. A desperate, needy sound fills the room, and I realize it's coming from me as I'm frantically sucking and thrusting my hips into the powerful jet. Case pulls my hair hard, and finally, *finally* starts thrusting into my mouth, pumping into me hard and fast and I'm not sure I've ever felt anything so fucking amazing in my life.

His rhythm falters and he gasps, "I'm gonna come, pull off if- ohhh."

The first spurt of his release floods my mouth, and I pull back just enough so I don't choke, but I swallow frantically, not wanting to let one drop go to waste. God, he tastes so good. How have I lived my entire life and never known how fucking amazing it is to give a blowjob? Michele would do it for me occasionally, but it wasn't something she enjoyed all that much. But this. My god, how is giving head just as good as receiving it?

Case shudders and pushes me away gently as the waves of his orgasm slow down. I release his cock from my mouth, still kneeling in front of him in the water, resting my head on his inner thigh as we catch our breaths, and he runs his fingers gently through my damp hair.

"Come up here," he whispers after a few moments. I raise myself out of the water, shivering as the cold air hits me, and he grabs my hips, then lies back so I'm on top of him, his feet still dangling in the hot tub. I shift so I'm straddling him, taking some of my body weight onto my knees. He pulls my head down and takes my mouth in a fierce kiss. I moan when I think about how he's tasting himself on me. Again, how have I never realized how hot that is?

I'm hard as a rock, and he reaches a hand between our bodies, still plundering my mouth from below as he jerks me fast and hard. It only takes a few strokes before my muscles tense and I come as hard as I ever have, covering his abs with ropes of my release. When it's over I collapse onto him, my come smearing all over our bellies as I catch my breath.

"Jesus, Matt. You're telling me that's the first blowjob you've ever given?" he sounds incredulous, and I take it for the compliment it is with a grin.

"Scout's honor," I smirk, and he snorts.

"That was not a Boy Scout level blowjob. That was definitely Eagle Scout caliber."

It's my turn to snort as I reply. "Funny, I don't remember there being a badge for that."

We lie together for a few more minutes, but as our bodies cool down, we both start feeling the cold. "Should we clean up out here and go inside?" He asks, and I nod.

We put the cover back on the hot tub, grab the pile of wet towels, and close up the room. Slipping into our identical fuzzy robes and slippers, he leans in to kiss me. "I'm going to shower and then I'm going to hit the sack, if that's okay with you?" he asks, searching my eyes. He doesn't invite me to shower with him, or show any sign that he wants to sleep together, so I paste a lazy grin on my face to hide the twinge of disappointment that slices through me.

"I'm going to do the same. It's getting late. I'll see you in the morning." I wink at him, and he smiles.

"Sleep well, Matthew. I know I will." Before I can walk away, he reaches out and kisses me softly. No tongue, just a sweet, gentle goodnight kiss.

Bringing my fingertips to my lips, I can still feel his kiss when I step into the shower a few minutes later.

I don't know where this is going to go. I just hope I'll be ready to deal with whatever the fallout is when it comes to an end.

Chapter Twelve

Case

The bedroom is cold, and the wind gusts are so strong I can feel the house shiver as they buffet the cabin, but underneath the cozy quilt I'm toasty warm. Last night, I was sure my decision to sleep alone was the best choice after the earth-shattering encounter with Matt in the hot tub. I wanted to make sure we didn't cross any lines, clarifying that this is just an extended hookup, nothing else. But this morning I'm wishing he was here beside me so I could pull his warm body against mine and rub up against him. Unfortunately, nature doesn't seem to care how comfortable this bed is, or how pleasurable my fantasy about Matt will be, because my bladder is complaining loudly. Sighing, I throw back the quilt and roll out of bed.

After I'm done in the bathroom, I take a peek out the window, and am stunned at the amount of snow that's already on the ground while it continues to fall hard and fast. Every once in a while, the howling wind lifts swirls of the white powder into the air, making it jump and twirl like a ballet dancer.

The thick, white blanket covers everything, softening all the edges and blending everything together so it's hard to distinguish one lump from another.

My stomach lets out an aggravated growl, so I throw on an old pair of track pants and a warm sweatshirt, and head to the living room. The scene outside the big picture windows is much the same as from my bedroom, cold and gray but strangely beautiful.

Once I get a fire started, I go to the kitchen and check out the fridge, which is bursting with food. Matt was not kidding when he said he brought enough stuff for a month.

I find eggs and a package of bacon, and then search around for bowls and frying pans.

The bacon is sizzling and I'm starting on the eggs when I hear a startled noise from behind me. Turning around, I find Matt standing at the edge of the kitchen, looking adorably bleary-eyed, his hair sticking up at an odd angle.

"You made breakfast?" he says through a yawn, rubbing his eyes like a little kid.

"I figured since you've been kind enough to let me crash your vacation, I could at least thank you with breakfast." I grin at him. "Well, that and I was freaking starving."

He chuckles in response, stepping toward the coffee machine and grabbing the mug I'd set out for him.

After doctoring up his coffee with the vanilla creamer I found in the fridge, he takes a seat at the kitchen island and we're silent as the eggs cook and he downs his caffeine. As soon as the eggs are done, I slide his plate over to him and take a seat beside him with my own.

"This is delicious," Matt says a few minutes later. "Thanks for cooking. If there was one thing didn't expect on this trip, it was a personal chef."

I laugh. "I'm no Anthony Bourdain, but bacon and eggs I can do."

He smiles again, and there are a few more moments of silence. He puts his fork down and takes a sip of coffee.

"So, are you... doing okay?" I ask.

He nods. "Yeah, I actually am. I think."

I chuckle. "You think? If you're hiding a gay-freak-out under that casual exterior, I say 'bravo', because your performance is flawless."

He chuckles. "Nope, no morning-after panic. I'm not that good an actor." He takes another big gulp of coffee. "My therapist is worth his weight in gold. It took a while to figure it out, but I think 'bisexual' is the label that fits me best, at least at the moment."

"So, how do you feel about it?"

"I'm okay with it. Honestly, I'm better than okay. I've started believing stumbling into these huge discoveries about myself is a good thing, not something I should regret. The idea that a person's sexuality can change is new to me, but it makes sense. Especially with the new things they're discovering about how our brains change physically as a result of our experiences."

"Now you're speaking my language," I grin at him. "Brain science is fascinating, and I agree with you. I think our sexuality can change over time. My guess is that it's at least partly because of physical changes. The recent research on how we can build new neural pathways in our brains is amazing, and there's still so much we don't know." I could literally talk about this topic for hours, but since I don't want to put Matt to sleep, I shelve the brain science talking points for now.

"Right. The other thing is, even if I was attracted to men when I was younger, I don't think I would have even noticed it. It wouldn't have occurred to me that I could be anything other than straight."

I nod, taking another swallow of my coffee. "I'm happy you're okay with it. Not everyone would be."

He shrugs. "It took a little time to get there, I admit. Not because of any internalized homophobia, I don't think. It was just that seeing myself as 'not straight' was so unfamiliar." He pauses for a second before continuing.

"The one thing I worry about is whether coming out would affect the company or my business relationships. And I haven't told my ex or my kids. There's been no reason, since I haven't dated anyone I wanted to see more than once."

"Right," I say. Hearing him admit he has reservations about coming out to his family and business makes me feel anxious and disappointed. And I don't even want to examine why that is right now.

"I get it. And forgive the psychology-speak, but it's a process. You sound like you're doing great. It takes time." I give him an encouraging smile.

"I'll get there." He returns my smile. "Like I said, if I were to meet someone I wanted to be with, I wouldn't want to hide. But until that happens...." He lets his voice trail off as we stare into each other's eyes.

Chapter Thirteen

Matthew

We finish breakfast in comfortable silence, and work together to clean up the kitchen when we're done.

"So, what about you?" I ask Case. "Never been married or in a serious relationship?"

"No, no. I'm definitely not a relationship guy." He says without turning around to meet my eyes. "I've dated people for a few months at a time, back when I was younger, but they never went any further. And I had a couple of experiences that showed me relationships are not my thing."

"Oh. Bad breakup?" I ask sympathetically.

"No, nothing like that." He clears his throat. "When I was about 20, I was in a serious car accident that left me with some serious injuries and PTSD. And then when I was 32, my youngest brother died."

"Oh god, Case, I'm so sorry. I didn't realize." I stammer, but he smiles reassuringly.

"It's fine. How would you know? Anyway, those two experiences made it crystal clear to me how fragile life is. I'm naturally a cautious person, and after those experiences.." He hesitates, searching for the right words. "I'm uncomfortable with how I feel when I'm in a relationship. I've seen how fast things can change, and how quickly someone you love can be gone from your life." He looks at me with a half-smile on his lips that doesn't reach his eyes.

"That makes sense," I say. "I'm so sorry about your brother. That must have been so devastating."

Case looks into his mostly empty coffee mug. "It was. We all miss him, but we talk about him a lot. It keeps him with us, you know? I like talking about him. It's just not always easy to do."

I hesitate for a moment. "I'd love to hear about him. I mean, if you want to tell me."

He smiles and gets up to refill our coffees. "Like I told you last night, I'm one of five kids. My brother Michael is the oldest. Then there's me, followed by my sister Olivia, and the twins Jacob and Danny. I'm almost ten years older than the twins—they were a 'happy surprise' my parents like to say." He smirks. "My dad is pretty outdoorsy, and Danny took after him. His favorite thing was back country skiing. When he was 23, he was on a ski trip with a group of friends in Colorado. They were all experienced and knew what they were doing, but they got caught in an avalanche. Danny didn't make it."

"Oh my god, Case." I cover my mouth with one hand. He's sitting on the bar stool beside me, and I put my hand on his knee. "I'm so sorry. What a terrible loss."

"Thank you," he says with a wistful smile, his eyes shiny with tears. He covers my hand with his, and my heart speeds up.

"It was hard for everyone, not only our family, but the friends who were with him as well. They were all so overcome with guilt, even though there was nothing they could have done. Danny was just in the wrong place at the wrong time."

Case clears his throat and takes a sip of his coffee. "Dan's death, combined with the PTSD after my car accident, showed me how fragile life is. Not to give you an existential crisis or anything, it's just-" He stops for a moment and takes a sip of coffee before he takes a breath and continues. "It's probably a huge cliché, but I think of life as a giant casino. Every day, every minute of our lives, we're rolling the dice, taking our chances, and when our number comes up, it's all over. I hope that doesn't sound too weird?" he says softly, and I can see the vulnerability in his eyes. "I just don't know if I could survive losing another person I loved as much as my brother."

I shake my head. "Not weird at all."

"So, anyway, I don't date. I have my family, and some amazing friends who I love, but as for relationships, I keep things simple. I rarely see people more than once. It keeps both of us from catching feelings."

"Right," I say. I understand why he would feel that way, but the stab of pain that slices through my belly tells me that as crazy as the idea is, there was a part of me that thought it was possible for Case and me to be more than an extended hookup. But that fantasy dissolves like dust in the wind.

Chapter Fourteen

Matthew

After we clean up the breakfast dishes, I settle myself into the couch and turn on the TV where the local news station is covering the storm, which, apparently, isn't even half over. The winds are expected to get even stronger tonight and they say most of the region needs to be prepared to be without power for several days. This does not sound like what I had planned for my relaxing getaway. But the thought of being in this little bubble with Case, where no one else can reach us, makes the idea a lot more appealing.

"Wow", he says. "I guess they're pretty serious about this one, huh?" He's standing next to the picture window sipping his coffee while watching. He gestures to the neatly stacked pile of firewood beside the hearth. "Do you know if that's all the firewood we have?" he asks.

"No, there's plenty more outside," I say. "Maybe we should bring some in before things get worse?"

"Yeah, let's do that."

So we bundle up and head outside into the storm. There's an ominous feeling in the air, and it's so cold it almost hurts to breathe. While the snow has slowed down for the moment, there are still a few lacy snowflakes drifting slowly down from the gray sky. There's so much snow, our cars look like oddly shaped, giant marshmallows, and the soft white blanket is so thick that it muffles any noise, making it feel peaceful.

We tromp across the big yard, and I show Case where I found the extra firewood and also point out the generator. After what feels like about two hundred trips back and forth across the yard with heavy armfuls of wood, we finally decide our next load will be the last. I walk toward the house ahead of Case, sticking to the trench we've already cut through the knee-deep snow. I feel like I'm in pretty good shape for my age, but nearly an hour of plowing through two feet of snow has me winded and sweating. I glance over my shoulder to say something when I realize Case isn't behind me anymore.

"What the hell?" I mutter. Still holding the heavy load of wood, I turn to look for him when I'm hit squarely in the face with a very soft but extremely cold ball of snow.

I let out an un-manly squeal and drop my pile of firewood into the snow, bending over immediately to make some of my own snowballs for retaliation. I hear Case cackle, and see him disappear around the side of the main house. I have no idea how he got ahead of me without my noticing, but I don't care, as I chase him through the snow, armed with a few hastily put together snowballs, my earlier exhaustion gone. The snow is so light and powdery it doesn't stick together well, so it doesn't make good snowballs, but on the upside, getting one in the face doesn't hurt. It's just a shock to the system.

Turning the corner where I saw him disappear, I realize I've made a rookie mistake, charging into battle without doing any recon, because he's lying in wait for me. As soon as I get around the corner, I'm hit three times in succession with more soft bombs that explode in a cascade of white when they hit my jacket, my hat, and the side of my head.

"Oh man, now it's on," I yell at his retreating back as he hurries to round the far corner. I move fast when I'm motivated, and I'm highly competitive, so by the time he looks over his shoulder to see how far behind him I am, I'm close enough to target him squarely in the face, getting him as good as he got me moments earlier. He lets out a strangled-sounding yelp and keeps running, but I can hear him laughing as I pause to reload with more ammunition.

Our war goes on for a while, both of us getting in some great shots, and we're both breathing hard and drenched in sweat with red cheeks and runny noses when we decide to call a truce. Case shucks off his gloves and hat, and steam rises from his damp hair. He grins at me, extends both arms out to his sides, and lets his body fall backwards into the soft snow. He opens and closes his arms and legs as if he's doing horizontal jumping jacks, making a perfect snow angel. Gasping with laughter, I flop down beside him, taking off my own hat and gloves and enjoying the feeling of the cold snow against my hot skin.

Fuck me sideways, he is gorgeous. With his red cheeks and bright blue eyes against his pale skin, I can see a few light freckles sprinkled across his nose and cheeks that I haven't noticed before, and all I can think about is how I want to kiss each one of them and trace them with my tongue.

Bloody hell. I want to kiss him. I want to feel his lips against mine, his tongue in my mouth, his skin pressed against me. My mind flashes back to last night and the feeling of his smooth skin, lightly covered with fine, blond hair, so different from my own, which is covered in coarse dark hair. I remember our first night together, and how different it felt to be with a man. So different, but so amazing. I can feel his whole body pressed tight against my own even as we're lying here in the snow, fully dressed. My breath hitches when I look into his eyes and find their icy blue color has darkened with lust, and they look almost indigo.

Shifting closer to me, he lifts his hand and traces his fingers over my jaw as gently as a butterfly kiss before curling his hand around the back of my neck and pulling me into a kiss. Leaning in, he presses his mouth to mine, softly at first until I open for him and he slides his tongue into my mouth, pulling a groan from my throat. *Fuck the man can kiss.* Suddenly, I'm struck by the thought that for the first time ever, I don't have to be the one in charge during sex. I can just enjoy it and let him set the pace. Case seems to be naturally comfortable leading in the bedroom, and that thought settles me even more. I've never thought about it, but I think I've always wanted a partner who's more dominant in bed, and right now Case feels fucking perfect.

He slides his hand from the back of my neck into my hair as our tongues tangle together, hot and wet. Keeping our mouths fused, he rolls us so I'm on my back in the snow, with him lying on top of me, still kissing me like I'm the last man on earth. I can feel the heat from his body even through all of our layers, and the contrast with the icy snow at my back is delicious.

His sandy-colored beard is delightfully rough against my neck as he kisses his way over my jaw to the sensitive spot behind my ear, and I gasp when he gently sucks my earlobe into his hot mouth. I shiver when he traces the shell of my ear with the tip of his tongue, his breath is hot against my skin.

"Fuck, you taste so good," he whispers, taking my earlobe into his mouth again. "But if we don't get inside soon, we might end up buried under three feet of snow."

I snort with laughter. The snow is falling faster again, and it looks like we're going to get another couple of feet overnight.

He grins as we both sit up. "I haven't had a good snowball fight since I was a kid, that was awesome!" He gets up and dusts the powdery snow off himself, and then extends his hand to me, pulling me to my feet.

As we gather up the wood we dropped earlier, I realize how much fun I'm having. I can't even remember another time when I've had this much fun with another person. To be honest, lately I feel like I've forgotten how to even have fun, but something about Case reminds me. And I like it. A lot.

After we get back inside and warm up with more coffee, we spend the rest of the afternoon relaxing while the snow falls. We read, we each take a nap, and later in the afternoon I break out another bottle of red wine and we nibble on meat and cheese in front of the crackling fire.

As predicted, the cabin loses power part way through the afternoon when the wind picks up, and we're left with only the fire and candles for light since we've agreed we should use only the generator to power the fridge and freezer. But the afternoon bleeds into the evening and the feeling of being in our own world is amplified because there's only firelight.

"Can I ask you something?" Case says. We're lying at opposite ends of the couch, our legs tangled together, each of us covered by a cozy quilt. We're both feeling pleasantly dreamy from the wine and the warmth of the fire, and I don't remember the last time I felt so relaxed.

"Of course."

"It sounds like you and Michele are still really close, I'm just wondering why you split up."

"There's really no big story," I tell him. "Just another stereotypical, middle-age divorce where the woman raised the kids and the man worked outside the home." I let out a sigh. Even though I know it's the right choice to split up, it still feels like a failure. "I was raised in a traditional family, and even though I didn't consciously believe it, on some deeper level, I believed my job took priority over everything else. I wouldn't say I took her for granted, but I would say that on some deep, subconscious level, I felt like what she was doing wasn't as important as what I was doing. I would say all the right things, but when it came down to actions, I fell way short. It's ten kinds of fucked up, but that's the gist of it.

"Do you still love her?" he asks nonchalantly.

"I'll always love Michele. We were best friends before we got married, and to be honest, we were more friends than lovers for most of our marriage. But we haven't been 'in love' for a very long time. I'm not even sure we ever were."

Case smiles. "I'm glad you're still able to be friends."

"I am too. She's a great mom to my kids, and like I said, we've been best friends for more than twenty-five years. But I'm excited about the possibilities in front of me now. For the first time in a long time, I don't know what the future is going to bring, but I can't wait to find out."

We spend the rest of the evening talking about everything and nothing as the snow falls. Tomorrow is Christmas Eve, so I'm thankful we discovered the cabin's wired internet connection before we lost power, since we were able to to send emails letting people know we're safe and warm but will definitely be trapped here for a few more days.

By the time the fire has died down it's late, and we're cuddled together on the couch, wrapped in blankets, both of us slightly tipsy from all the red wine. Case stretches underneath me, yawning, and I raise my head to look at him sleepily.

"I think this body of mine needs to hit the sack," he smiles. "Not that snuggling with you on this couch isn't delightful, but if I spend all night out here I'll regret it tomorrow."

I yawn and shimmy up his body to plant a soft kiss on his mouth.

"I'm ready for bed, too. But it's awfully cold in here." I snuggle deeper into him. "I think it's only sensible if we share a bed, don't you think? So we can share body heat?"

He grins at me, his eyes twinkling in the firelight. "I absolutely agree. Anything else would be irresponsible. Your place or mine."

"Mine," I say confidently. "I've got the bigger bed and the nicer bathroom." I roll off him and take a minute to blow out a couple of the candles scattered around before grabbing his hand and pulling him up.

"Well, lead the way to your private lair, then." His grin is wolfish as he smiles down at me.

Chapter Fifteen

Case

Waking up in bed with Matt on Christmas Eve feels surreal. It's still snowing like crazy outside and it's cold as fuck in the bedroom, but with both of us cuddled under the quilt, it's cozy and comfortable in bed. I scooch closer to him, wrapping an arm around his waist and pressing my chest to his back. He gives a little sigh and snuggles back into me, pressing his perfect ass into my morning wood. I plant a soft kiss on his shoulder and let myself drift, enjoying my dreamy, half-awake state. How wonderful would it be to wake up like this every morning?

A couple of hours later, I'm wide awake and Matt's still sawing logs beside me. I decide to get up and make sure the living area of the house is nice and toasty before he wakes up. Throwing on a heavy sweatshirt and flannel sleep pants, I pad out to the living room, where I can see in the gray light of dawn that the snow is still coming down hard.

"Brr." I mutter to myself as I set about starting the fire. A few minutes later, I hear the soft shuffling of slippers on the hardwood and Matt appears from down the hallway. He's so adorable in the mornings. His hair is all mussed up, and he rubs his eyes like a little kid. I want to wrap my arms around him, cover him in kisses and take him back to the bedroom.

"Coffee should be ready. It's on the counter," I say.

He smiles at me sleepily. "Man, you are awfully convenient to have around. If you keep this up, I'm never going to want to take another vacation without you."

I know he's just joking, but my stomach lurches anyway. Vacations together. Visions of a tropical beach, maybe with one of those over-the-water-cabanas float through my mind. Then I remember this morning's half-awake dream about sleeping in the same bed with him every night and waking up together every morning. *What am I doing? I don't want a relationship*. This whole thing with Matt has gone much further than a hookup. And I don't know what to think about that. Shaking my head, I push the complicated feelings down and follow Matt into the kitchen.

We drink our first coffees in companionable silence, and when I'm done I get up and stretch. "I'm going to pop outside and make sure there's enough gas in the generator," I say.

"Okay," Matt says. "I'll start breakfast while you do that." He gets up and reaches out to grab my empty mug while at the same time leaning over and planting a sweet kiss on my cheek. I freeze, feeling my heart stutter in my chest as he carries on with what he's doing, grabbing a sponge to wipe up the drops from the French press. He's humming under his breath, and the routine domesticity of the scene hits me square in the chest. But I'm not freaking out about how domestic it feels. I'm freaking out because of how much I love it. It just feels right, and that's the terrifying part.

As I trudge around the corner of the house in the biting wind and snow to get to the generator, I decide to put everything aside for now. Whatever it is I'm feeling for Matt, I can figure out in a day or two. Today is Christmas Eve, and I want to enjoy the day with him. Regardless of what happens between us in the future, this will be a Christmas we'll both remember, and I want the memory to be a good one.

When I get back inside, Matt's standing at the stove working on breakfast. I catch him by surprise when I sneak up behind him, wrapping my arms around his waist.

"Merry Christmas Eve, by the way," I whisper in his ear, which earns me a sweet giggle. "I was thinking we should do a little decorating today." I grin at him when he gives me a confused look.

"Merry Christmas Eve to you too, but what do you have in mind for decorating? I'm not sure I'm up for digging up one of those big trees in the yard and setting it up in the living room, all Clark Griswold, *Christmas Vacation* style."

I snort. "As much fun as that would *obviously* be, that's not what I was thinking. Have you ever made paper snowflakes? And what about popcorn garlands?"

He raises an eyebrow. "I know about paper snowflakes, but what did you say about popcorn?"

I laugh. "My mom used to have us do it as kids. She would give each of us a big sewing needle and a long piece of thick thread. We would poke the needles through the pieces of popcorn and string them along, so they looked like garlands." I laugh as the memories of Christmases long past wash over me. "It's a brilliant idea, actually. The kid who made the longest popcorn string would get a prize, so we would all sit there for ages with our bowls of popcorn and needle and thread. It was probably the longest quiet stretch she'd get for two solid weeks while we were out of school."

Matthew laughs. "That sounds super cute, and no, we never did anything like that. But I'm in. Let's see what we can find around here to make this place a little more Christmassy."

Chapter Sixteen

Case

The rest of the day seems to pass in the blink of an eye. Matt finds a bunch of Christmas lights, and a tabletop Christmas tree. Since the power is still out, the lights aren't of much use to us, but we set up the little tree, and make paper snowflakes. He also tracks down a sewing kit, so we pop some corn the old-fashioned way, on the stovetop, and then compete to see who can make the longer popcorn string in an hour. Matt wins easily, but I maintain that my loss was only because he kept distracting me by looking adorable.

Almost before I realize it, the sun has set, and it's dark again. The snow has picked up, but according to the local radio station we're listening to, since both our phones have died, this band of weather is one of the last to pass through. Christmas day looks like it will be bright and sunny. Road crews will work 24/7, to get the roads and highways back open as soon as possible, which means our time together is coming to an end quickly.

Ignoring the way my stomach clenches when I think about leaving, I press my lips to his temple as he leans against my chest on the couch. "How do you feel about an extra-special Christmas Eve dinner of tomato soup and grilled cheese?"

He smiles up at me, his eyes twinkling like he's some kind of hot Santa Claus. "Sounds like a perfect Christmas Eve feast." He stretches up to kiss me. Feeling my cock harden against him, he breaks the kiss and gives me a mischievous smile. "Let's get to that feast, and when we're finished, I plan to have a different sort of feast later." He waggles his eyebrows.

"Count me in for that." I waggle my eyebrows at him. After giving him a peck on the nose, I head to the kitchen and start putting together gourmet grilled cheese sandwiches. Naturally, he didn't just bring a can of boring old Campbell's tomato soup with him. No, he brought some kind of gourmet tomato bisque something or other, but it looks divine as I pour it into a saucepan to heat it up.

Matt pours us more wine and fixes us a beautiful cheese plate to have with dinner, and when we're done, we carry all of it into the living room. Setting up our little picnic on the coffee table, we sit beside each other on the floor, and dig in. He lets out a sexy-as-fuck groan as he bites into the grilled cheese, nearly causing me to forget dinner entirely so I can feast on him right now.

"Jesus fuck, that's the best grilled cheese sandwich I've had in my life," he says, his eyes closed. "What kind of black magic did you use to make this?"

"It's all in the ingredients. And you provided the best. But there may also be a little trick in how you toast the bread." I grin at him, taking a bite of my own sandwich and damn, he's right, it *is* good. "It's a family secret, though. I could tell you, but then I'd have to kill you."

He barks out a laugh before taking another bite, emitting another groan. "If they have these sandwiches in the afterlife, I'd be totally fine with that. This shit is one hundred percent to die for."

Once we're finished eating, we lean back on the couch, still sitting on the floor. We're both feeling pleasantly fuzzy, after finishing today's second bottle of wine. I don't want to know what time it is, because I'll start calculating how much time we have left together before the real world finds us. Instead, I lean over to and give him a gentle kiss. Draining the last of the wine from his glass, he places it on the coffee table before taking mine and doing the same. Standing up, he extends a hand to me. "Come on, beautiful one. I'm hungry for that second feast we mentioned earlier." He gives me a look that damn near melts my underwear off, his gaze trailing up and down my body.

"I'm good with that idea," I grin at him, hopping up off the floor eagerly.

We make our way down the hallway to the primary suite at the end, and when we walk in, I realize he snuck away at some point and set up a bunch of candles all around the room, bathing it in the warm glow of firelight. It's like stepping into an enchanted realm. Closing the door quietly behind us, he turns to me, and without saying a word, starts undressing me slowly and methodically. His movements are precise and unhurried and as he removes each piece of clothing, he runs his hands over every inch of my newly exposed skin. With the heat out for the last few days, the room is cold and I shiver as he drops to his knees to take off my pants and briefs. Goosebumps rise on my skin as he looks up at me from where he's kneeling at my feet, with my cock exactly at his eye level. Running his hands up my flanks, he stops at my hips, and without breaking eye contact, runs his tongue up my length, causing a gasp to escape me.

His eyes are molten lava as he gets gracefully to his feet and leads me to the bed. Not only has he taken the time to light the candles, he's changed the sheets on the bed. Earlier, the sheets were chic and stylish, matching the rest of the bedroom perfectly. Matt has replaced them with soft flannel sheets, complete with Christmas illustrations. Big, chunky Santas, along with a few elves and some reindeer, dance across a white background, making me giggle. Taking a closer look, I realize there's something a little different about these Santas. They're Santa-bears. But not polar bears. These particular Santa-Bears are a gay elf's dream, each one outfitted in a different version of Santa-style jock straps, harnesses, and leather-wear.

I let out a huge belly laugh and climb onto the bed to get a closer look.

"Oh my god, where did you find these? They're amazing!" I can barely speak, I'm laughing so hard, as he stands beside the bed grinning. "I found them in a closet earlier." He laughs. "Aren't they fantastic?"

"I fucking love them." I run my hands across the soft fabric, looking at all the different versions of kinky gay Santa and all his elves.

"Maybe I can ask Hunter where they got them," Matt grins as he quickly sheds his clothes and jumps into bed beside me. I immediately pull up the soft sheets and comforter, and we wrap our arms around each other, burrowing deep into our little nest, giggling and laughing as we run our hands over each other's bodies.

A few minutes later, the cute sheets are forgotten. My entire being is completely focused on the deliciously naked man lying on top of me, feeling like he belongs there. Our bodies are stretched out against each other, and his weight pressing down on my body feels perfect.

Chapter Seventeen

Matthew

C ase's hands trace gentle patterns on my back, and I can't help but notice how well we fit together as we kiss. He's bigger than me, but I don't feel small, I feel safe. The way he looks at me makes me feel almost cherished. Case turns us again so I'm on my back, but he's stretched out on his side beside me, one of his hands roaming over my chest. Leaning over, he sucks one nipple into his mouth and I groan and arch my back. Holy Christ it feels good. I never realized my nipples were so sensitive.

"Case, I whisper as he nibbles on my collarbone. "I want you inside me. I want you to fuck me tonight." He stills and pulls back so he can see my face.

"Yeah?" he whispers?

I nod. "God, yes. That first night was amazing, but I was so overwhelmed it's almost a blur. I want you to take me again, and I want to remember all of it. I need to."

He groans and falls on me. "I want that too, so much," he whispers before crushing his mouth onto mine in a searing kiss that leaves no doubt he wants this as much as I do.

I reach over to grab the supplies I left in the nightstand earlier, knowing I wanted this to happen tonight. We only have a couple more nights left together, and I don't want to waste any time.

Case kisses me so intensely it makes my eyes roll back in my head and whimper as I rub my hard cock against the thigh he has pressed between my legs.

A few moments later, he sits back and grabs a pillow, helping me arrange it under my hips. "I want you to be perfectly comfortable," he whispers into my mouth, and I chuckle.

"I'll be more comfortable when you put your dick inside me," and he groans.

"Fuck I love Dirty Talking Matt," he grins.

He grabs the lube from where it's lying beside me, and squeezes some onto his fingers, but before he touches me, he uses his other hand to gently spread my legs open, his eyes roaming over my body. "Fuuuck, you look so good," he whispers.

I feel like I should be embarrassed, but I'm not. It's probably because of the naked hunger in his eyes when he leans down to press his nose to the crease of my groin and inhales deeply. "Fuck, you smell so good too," he groans. And when he licks a stripe up my crack between my cheeks and over my hole, I nearly jump off the bed, letting out a surprised yelp. "Fuck, you taste good, too. I'm sorry, though, is that too much?" He rubs my abdomen soothingly with his non lube-covered hand.

"No, I was just surprised. I'm good. Feels good." I whisper. I'm fast approaching the point where I won't be able to form sentences. "Case I need you inside me, I need you to fill me with your cock," I whimper and he groans.

"You say the sweetest things." He grins down at me, making me laugh. I love how we shift between seriousness and laughter. Even during sex, we're so comfortable with each other. I shimmy my hips. "If you don't get inside me right fucking now, I'm going to get a lot less sweet."

"Mmm, patience, lover," we're getting there." He gives me an evil smile as he takes a lube-covered finger and gently presses against my entrance. I arch my back again and press down into him as he slides it further inside me.

"Oh god yes, more, like that," I rasp as he moves and his finger brushes my prostate, nearly making me blow everything right there as my vision whites out for a second.

He slides another finger inside me, refusing to be hurried along, no matter how much I beg. "We need to make sure you're ready for me. Because I'm not going to be gentle with you." he whispers, and I groan.

Finally, after what feels like a lifetime, he slides his fingers out and replaces them with his condom-covered cock. We both let out deep groans as he slips inside me without much resistance. Even with all the prep he insisted on, it burns, and I suck in my breath as he pauses, running his hands up and down my thighs, whispering gentle, soothing words. It only takes a minute before I'm grinding down on him, begging for more. He sinks deeper into me, filling me so much I almost can't breathe. I remember from that first night how this feeling changed from weirdly overwhelming to burning, aching need so fast, and sure enough, the same thing happens this time.

"Move, please, move," I beg urgently, and for once he doesn't tease or argue, but moves inside me. Slowly at first, but soon it isn't enough. "I need more, faster, please." I whine. He obliges, pulling almost all the way out of me before slamming back in, hard. I moan, taking one hand and bracing myself against the headboard, so I don't bang my head with the force of his thrusts. I wrap my other hand around my cock, jerking myself in time with Case's thrusts. The need and pressure inside me grows until I feel like I might explode with need.

"Case, I can't wait, I'm gonna come."

"Do it," he demands. "Come for me, now." The commanding tone of his voice pushes me right over the edge with a scream. Case tenses at the same time, and we fall off that cliff together, the sensations hitting me like a tidal wave and causing my vision to close in.

"Oh god, oh god, oh my god," I gasp as Case collapses onto me. His heart is pounding so hard I can feel it against my own chest as we lie together in a sweaty, come-covered heap while we catch our breaths.

After a few minutes, he goes into the bathroom and cleans us both up with a warm towel when he returns. Then he climbs back into bed and I curl into him, my head resting on his chest.

Gently dragging my fingers through his chest hair, I let myself drift on the pleasant endorphins, feeling dreamy and blissed out.

He shifts underneath me, and I lift my head so I can see his face. His eyes are earnest when he searches mine. "Matthew, that was... amazing. It's never been like that for me. I-" he swallows and looks away briefly before returning his eyes to mine. "I've never experienced that kind of- connection.. I don't want to freak you out.. I just..."

"I know, Case. I feel the same." I plant a gentle kiss on his lips before resting my head back on his chest. The steady rhythm of his heart beneath my ear grounds me. I'm not sure what's happening between us. It's something I'm not sure either of us is ready to face.

As I'm drifting off to sleep, I finally admit to myself that I'm all in with this man. If he wants me, I'm there for him. I've been trying to hold part of myself back, but tonight I gave him everything. I don't know how, or even if it could ever work, but there's no holding back for me now. He's got my heart, and there is no guarantee he'll give me his in return.

Chapter Eighteen

Case

Christmas morning dawns bright and sunny. For the first time since I've been here, the sunshine is pouring through the bedroom window. It feels amazing, and I take a moment to stretch like a cat before fully waking up. Matt stirs beside me, and I smile as he lets out a noise that sounds like a purr as he also stretches in the sunlight. He is so fucking cute when he first wakes up. This is my favorite time with him: before he's put on his mask for the day to become the perfect corporate titan that the rest of the world sees, he's just Matt. Sweet, goofy, slightly insecure, and kind. He's amazing. I feel like my heart is expanding when I look at him, like I'm the Grinch or some shit.

My heart grows two sizes. He blinks at me sleepily, and a soft smile appears on his face. "Merry Christmas," he murmurs.

"Merry Christmas to you." I lean over and plant a kiss on him. Last night was incredible, and looking at him this morning, I have no idea how I'm going to let him go in a few days.

"MMmph, morning breath," he mumbles against my mouth.

"I don't give a tiny rat's ass about morning breath," I mumble back, and deepen the kiss. I can feel him hardening against me as I pull him close and roll us, so I'm lying on my back with him lying on top of me.

We lie there and trade leisurely kisses for a little while until he pushes away from me, and shifts so he's straddling my hips.

"This is going to sound cheesy, but it's Christmas, so I don't give a fuck," he says, running his palms over my chest. "This Christmas, my gift was the storm that brought you here. I'm so grateful you've been here for the last few days, Case. I don't know what's going to happen with us now that real life is catching up, but no matter what, you've made the last few days amazing, and I'll always remember them. Thank you."

My throat gets tight and I have to swallow down the tears that threaten to well up. I reach up and grab the back of his neck, pulling down into another kiss.

"I feel the same way." I say, looking up at him and I'm sure everything I'm feeling is written all over my face. "These few days have been amazing." I swallow hard again, and before I can talk myself out of it, I blurt out what I've been thinking. "This sounds crazy, especially coming from me," I start, "but I don't think I want this to be over when we leave. I know it won't be easy, living hundreds of miles apart, but maybe we can find a way to make a long-distance thing work?"

I can't believe I've just laid things on the line and told him I want more. Do I? And how the hell will it even work? It's not like either of us can up and move cities easily. But the thought of letting him go in the next couple of days and just returning to life as it was before... It doesn't even compute.. Whether I like it or not, my life isn't the same as it was. These last few days have changed everything.

Matt looks surprised when he realizes what I'm asking. But something in my belly warms when his face lights up with a smile.

"Really? You want to do a long distance thing?" He asks, looking both happy and puzzled.

I reach up and graze my fingertips across his jaw as he searches my eyes.

"I have no idea what it will look like. I don't know how we'll make it work, but I just know I don't want to let you go when we have to leave here. I... I think we can figure it out. If that's something you would want."

Matt chews on his bottom lip for a moment, like he always does when he's nervous, but then he meets my gaze, and his eyes tell me what I want to know.

"Of course I want to try. I don't know how it will work either. But we're two smart people. We can figure it out."

My gut unclenches, and I breathe out a sigh of relief. I'm still sitting with a mountain of uncertainty, but at least we both want to try. That's something.

Chapter Nineteen

Case

Although knowing Matt wants to continue our relationship after we leave the cabin is a huge relief, I'm still concerned about how we're going to make it happen. But that's a problem for the future. Right now, we have another day before we have to go our separate ways, so I'm going to focus all my energy on living in the moment.

"Hey, since it's finally stopped snowing, and we've been cooped up in here for days, want to head out for a hike today?" I suddenly blurt out. "I bet the trails around here will be absolutely stunning with all the snow."

Matt's eyes light up, and the warm feeling in my stomach that I'm quickly becoming addicted to spreads through my body. God, I love it when his smile reaches his eyes.

"I bet it's breathtaking out there. Let's do it! Breakfast first?" he asks, and I nod.

After we eat, we suit up, since even though the sun is shining, it's still bitterly cold. When we get outside, the sunshine almost feels sharp, like it's slicing through the snow. I pull in a long breath through my nose, blowing it out through my mouth and laughing as my breath clouds up the air and the little hairs in my nose feel like they're freezing together.

"God, I love the smell of the air up here," I say. "There's nothing like it. I understand why Danny loved it up here so much. I think he would have settled up here somewhere, eventually."

We're headed down toward the river. I don't plan to venture far up the trails, but if we're lucky, we'll be able to find a lookout where there will be stunning views. Wild, untamed, rugged mountains, slicing upwards, looking like they could tear a hole in the bright blue fabric of the sky.

Matt grabs my hand. "Yeah? You think he would have settled up here, even with your whole family in California?" he asks.

"Yeah. I can see him living in one of these little mountain towns, skiing in the winter and mountain biking and hiking in the summers. I bet he would run some kind of tour business, back country guiding, or heli-ski tours or something. He would have loved that. He was built for the outdoors, unlike most of the rest of our family." I smile wistfully.

Matt gives my hand a squeeze. "I love that you can think of him that way. That you can see him being happy and settled, doing something he loves."

We continue our walk, enjoying the sunshine and fresh air. The path leads us slowly upwards, and eventually we round a corner to find a spot exactly like I'd been hoping for. The path widens out, and there's a gap in the trees, opening up the view across the valley. Dozens of mountain peaks spread out in all directions, all topped with brilliant white powder that looks like someone has sprinkled them with icing sugar.

We stand together in silence for a few moments, holding hands and just enjoying the beauty that surrounds us. Matt leans into me, and I pull him closer, wrapping my arms around him, my front pressed to his back.

Suddenly, we hear a strange 'whumph' sound in the distance, causing my hackles to rise, suddenly on full alert. There's no mistaking that sound. There's an avalanche coming. Immediately, my body goes into panic mode and I'm desperate to see where it's coming from. But when I look toward the top of the hill directly behind us, everything looks calm and stable. Suddenly, Matt yanks my hand.

"Over there!" He's pointing toward the other side of the river, where there's a huge cloud of what looks like white smoke rising from the steep slope.

"Oh my god," I whisper. A huge chunk of snow has broken off and is sliding down the side of the mountain. It's way too far away to cause any danger for us, but my nervous system doesn't seem to have received that message. I can't catch my breath. *Shit.* I don't want to lose it and have a panic attack right here on the side of the mountain. Closing my eyes, I try to slow my breathing. I try to do the 'find five things' exercise to reconnect with my senses and calm down, but I can't get through it. Matt places his hand on my cheek, trying to get me to focus on him. "Case, it's okay. We're safe. It's on the other side of the river."

Taking deep breaths in through my nose and out through my mouth, I open my eyes slowly, looking immediately toward the slide zone. There's still snow floating around the area like flour in a baker's kitchen. If the noise the snow made when it first shifted hadn't plunged me immediately into 'fight or flight' mode, I would have been able to tell it was too far away to be a threat, but that sound is a powerful trigger for me.

"I'm okay," I say softly. Matthew's face is a mask of concern. I try to force a smile. "Can we head back now?" I whisper.

"Of course, baby. Let's go." Leaving his glove off, he grabs my hand again, leaving us skin to skin, and he leads us back to the path.

Chapter Twenty

Matthew

Less than an hour after we watched the avalanche on the other side of the river, we're back at the cabin. Case still looks as pale as the snow, and he was silent on the walk back. I feel terrible for him. When he heard that sound of the snow, he started shaking like a leaf and all the color drained from his face. He looks a little better now, but I'll won't be able to relax until I get him sitting comfortably on the couch with a hot drink in his hand.

I reach out to hug him once we've lost our heavy coats, and I realize he's drenched with sweat. The blue UCLA sweatshirt he's wearing is so wet it's practically dripping. His hair is wet too, and while he's got more color in his face than he did an hour ago, he still looks pale and shaken.

"Okay, honey, change of plans." I start. "I was going to get you settled on the couch with some hot chocolate and snacks, but you need a shower first. Come on."

He just looks at me and nods wordlessly, so I take his hand and pull him into the bathroom. I close the door and crank up the temperature on the shower until steam billows from behind the glass. Case is just standing there, his face almost blank, letting me fuss over him.

"Is it okay if I join you in there?" I ask him, and he smiles and nods, so I help him out of his clothes and ditch mine quickly. I step into the shower first, pulling him in behind me. Putting my arms around him, I turn us so the hot water cascades over his back and shoulders, and we stand like that for a few minutes. He buries his face in the crook of my neck and lets me slowly glide the soap over his back. Stepping back from him just enough to get a hand between us, I wash his front, taking tender care with all his parts. This feels so much more intimate than anything we've done, far more intimate than sex. Case is so vulnerable right now, and that he's letting me see him this way means more than I would have ever thought. A powerful urge to protect and care for him sits squarely in my chest, and I know without a doubt I would do anything in my power to keep him safe and shield him from this kind of pain.

Case

I'm a goddamn idiot. How did I not even think about the possibility of an avalanche? The day after a heavy snowfall can be one of the most dangerous times for avalanches. That's basic mountain safety. I should have at least had it in the back of my mind that seeing or hearing one was possible.

Taking another deep breath, I try to focus only on the physical sensation of the hot water coursing over my skin, and Matt's warm, wet skin pressed up against mine. His hands are gliding slowly up and down my back, soothing me, and I can feel some of the shock wearing off. I feel like Matt would be happy to stand here with me all day with me, just letting me feel what I need to. When I open my eyes, his face is full of concern. Placing a gentle kiss on his mouth, I whisper softly. "I'm feeling better. Thank you."

Reaching up, he caresses my cheek, and I press into him like a cat, loving the sensation. "Ready to get out?" I ask softly a moment later.

"If you are." He gives me another of those gentle smiles.

I reach back to shut off the water, and we each grab a huge, fluffy towel from the stack beside the shower.

I know it's ridiculous. Like seriously, utterly ridiculous, but I can't shake the feeling that maybe seeing the avalanche was some kind of sign. I don't even believe in that kind of shit. As a psychologist, I understand how our brains can trick us into believing stuff that isn't real. But even knowing all that, there's this niggling feeling at the back of my mind that I need to learn something from that avalanche today.

Even though I'm calmer now, my mind is still spinning with thoughts of my brother, and Matt, and what I should do now that I've realized my feelings. But I still have no idea how we're going to make things work.

After we dry off and get dressed, Matt leads me to the living room couch. "I'm going to make us some hot chocolate and snacks. You stay here."

"Oh, I can help-" I say, but he holds up a hand to stop me.

"Just let me take care of you, okay?" He says sternly. Then his voice softens. "It makes me feel good."

A few minutes later he's back with two steaming mugs of hot chocolate, which he sets on the coffee table, and then he zips back into the kitchen, returning with a big plate of cookies and other treats.

"Wow, where were you hiding those?" I laugh when I see the treats.

He grins. "I actually forgot I brought this stuff. Hazard of over-packing, I suppose." He grins.

He sits down next to me and we both sip our hot cocoa and munch on the cookies.

"So, are you okay?" he asks. "I understand if seeing an avalanche freaks you out."

"I'm okay," I sigh, and pause to blow on my hot chocolate before taking another sip. "I'm nervous and agitated, though. I should probably meditate or something. Not that I really know how." I roll my eyes.

"What are you agitated about?" he asks, taking another bite of cookie.

I breathe out a sigh. "True honesty? I'm nervous about us. I just can't see a realistic way for us to make a relationship work. But I don't want to lose you." His face is understanding, and he reaches for my hand, giving it a squeeze. "Matt, I've never felt anything like this before. My feelings for you are... really strong. But I've been so determined never to get attached to anyone for so long, part of me is resisting. My brain is coming up with every reason in the world why we could never work."

"I understand," he says softly.

"Losing Danny, and before that, the car accident I was in with Reed, showed me how fragile life is. No warning, just poof, someone you love more than anything can be gone one day. Other than Reed and my immediate family, I've wanted nothing to do with getting close to people, because the more people I care about, the greater the chances are that something could happen to them."

Matt nods, but remains quiet.

"I'm just really, fucking scared." I whisper to him, not meeting his eyes. "I'm not strong enough to survive losing someone I love again. And I'm worried about our chances of being successful in this relationship. Are we setting ourselves up to fail? And if we are, what's the point? Is it better to cut ourselves off now to spare the heartbreak? I don't know, Matt." I know I'm babbling, barely making sense. I lean forward and cover my face with my hands.

"Case, I'm scared too," he whispers, squeezing my hand again. "We may have to leave here tomorrow, but we don't have to have all the answers about our relationship right now. We have a lot to figure out, and we don't have all the information yet. Making a big decision without knowing all the info seems unwise, don't you think?"

I nod, trying really hard to let his sensible words sink in so I believe them.

He moves his hand soothingly up and down my leg, and when I look at him, I see someone who's confident and put together. Someone who knows how to take charge when a situation seems like it's falling apart. And it's hot as fuck.

"What I know is that we'll see each other as much as we can. Maybe next week we sit down with both our calendars and figure out good travel weeks. We can take this one day at a time for now. Does that make sense?"

"Right. Okay. I can do that." I say, letting out a big breath. As much as I want to believe it will be okay, it doesn't feel right to leave this place without a solid plan for the future. But I don't know what else we can do.

CHAPTER TWENTY-ONE

MATTHEW

The next morning is another lovely day of blue sky and just a few puffy white clouds. But I can't shake the dark cloud hanging over my head. I know I told Case I didn't think managing a long distance relationship would be a problem, but I'm nervous, too.

Reaching over to what has quickly become Case's side of the bed, I slide my hand over his taut ab muscles, watching as his eyelids flutter open, and he groans as he awakens. Pulling me into his arms, he whines, "I'm not ready yet. Just let me sleep for another few days. Then I'll be ready." I snuggle into his side, reluctant to get out of bed myself, but he has a flight booked back to San Diego later this afternoon, and since the roads have only just opened, there will probably be traffic.

"I know, I'm not ready either, sleepyhead. But come on. You don't want to miss your flight."

"Mm - maybe I do want to miss my flight." He makes a grab for me as I slide out of my side of the bed.

"Come on, if you hurry, maybe I'll still be in the shower when you get in there and we'll have to share." I waggle my eyebrows at him and he groans.

"Not fair, using sex as a bribe," he mumbles into the pillow.

I laugh. "Oh Case, I have three children. If there's one thing I know for sure, it's that bribery is a highly effective tool." I wait until he raises his head to look at me, and then I prance my naked ass into the bathroom, giving it a saucy little shake as I shoot him a sexy look over my shoulder, causing him to groan again and bury his face back into the pillow.

As I predicted, the bribery accomplishes the goal, and he meets me in the shower, which turns into an extended affair involving both of us getting clean, then getting dirty, followed by getting clean again. When we get into the kitchen a while later, I glance over at the oven, and to my surprise, the digital display is on, flashing 12:00 over and over. "Hey, the power's back on!" I exclaim.

He snorts. "Naturally, on the day we have to leave. Although I'm not complaining. We did pretty well without power, I think."

"I agree," I say, sliding my arms around his waist. "It wouldn't have been the same if we'd been able to have light and watch movies the whole time."

We spend the next couple of hours getting ready to leave, both struggling to hide our sadness. But after we've dug out both out cars, got Case packed up, loaded a few things into my SUV, and even done a little cleaning, there's nothing left to do. It's time for him to head out if he wants any chance of making his flight.

Standing in the driveway we worked together to shovel earlier, Case pulls me close one last time, nuzzling his face into the crook of my neck. I run my fingers through the hair on the back of his head and squeeze him as close to me as I can. There's no more room for smart-ass remarks. The moment we've been putting off and trying to avoid thinking about for the last few days is upon us.

"You feel so good," He whispers against my ear. He shaved this morning, and he feels different against my skin. Where there used to be rough stubble that felt so good scraping along my skin, now he's all smooth. I think I prefer him with a little scruff. My Case has sexy stubble, he's not this clean-shaven, college professor-y dude.

"I'll text you when I get to the airport, okay?" he whispers, and I nod against his chest, reluctant to let him go. "I'm going to miss you so much," he whispers, pressing his lips to my temple.

I look up at him, choking back the tears that threaten to spill over. I'm the one who convinced him that doing this whole thing long distance would be fine. I can't freak out now.

"I'll miss you too," I say softly. "But it will be fine."

He smiles, and his eyes are glassy as he takes his time giving me one last kiss. His mouth is gentle and warm against mine, one hand curled around the nape of my neck, and the other pressed firmly into the small of my back holding me tight to him.

"Goddamn," I whisper as we tear our mouths away from each other. "If you don't get out of here, I'm going to tear your clothes off and devour you right here in the driveway. I refuse to be responsible for you missing your flight and disappointing your family."

"Promises, promises," he grumbles, and slowly, reluctantly, we pull away from each other.

The car is already running, warming up in the cold, so Case gets himself settled in the driver's seat, and rolls down the window so I can lean in to plant one last kiss on him.

"Drive safely, okay?" I whisper, afraid that if I try to speak any louder, my voice will break.

Case nods. "You too."

I step back from the SUV as he puts it in gear and starts down the long driveway. I watch him until he reaches the road, and he sticks his arm out the driver's window, giving me one last wave as he turns and drives away.

My limbs feel like they're made of lead as I walk back into the cabin to finish packing and cleaning up. After a quick text exchange with Hunter, I learn the cleaners are coming tomorrow, so I don't have to do much other than gather up my stuff, but I end up doing a bunch of extra things, anyway. I'm just delaying going back to Seattle to a big empty house.

A couple of hours later, I pull the door shut behind me and make my way down the drive, following in the deep tracks left from when Case drove down. There's no one I'm leaving behind, and there's no one going to be there to greet me when I make it home, and goddamnit, that's one of the loneliest feelings I've ever experienced.

"Fuck," I mutter out loud, brushing away the annoying tears I keep finding on my cheeks.

The drive home is long, and traffic is a bitch. It's not surprising, but it certainly extends the length of my trip. A few hours in, I get a call from Case, as he's waiting for his flight to San Diego. We don't talk long since I'm driving, and after we disconnect I feel a pang of jealousy. At least Case has his parents and family there, while I've got my house and my job. I feel like those things might have been enough for me, even a few months ago, but right now, it just feels empty.

So, I do what I always do when I'm avoiding something. I think about work. And soon I'm able to lose myself in that. I love coming up with new game ideas. If I could do anything I wanted, I'd do nothing but sit around coming up with new game ideas.

A few hours later, I pull into my driveway. It's dark and cold, and there's plenty of snow that's fallen here in Seattle as well, but thankfully my caretakers have looked after clearing the driveway and walkways.

I shake my head ruefully as I pull into the garage and grab the bag with my personal stuff in it. I can unpack the rest tomorrow, but at the moment, all I can think of is a hot shower and falling into my bed.

Case is on his flight to San Diego, so after a hot shower, I crawl between my expensive sheets. I miss the ridiculous Santa Bear sheets from the cabin, and it makes me chuckle. I send Case a text letting him know I'm home safely and I miss him. And then after a little tv, I fall into a very restless sleep.

Chapter Twenty-Two

Case

I open my eyes slowly, and for a split second I'm back at the cabin, waking up next to Matt. The feeling that he should be right beside me is so strong that instinctively I reach over to grab him, but as soon as my hand hits the cool, soft sheets of my parents' guest bedroom I'm plunged back into reality as if someone poured a bucket of cold water over my head.

"Pffft." I blow out a long breath, trying to breathe out the anxiety and frustration building up in my chest. I didn't get in until late last night, and I was exhausted after the long drive, a flight, followed by another drive from San Diego up to Pasadena, so I went straight to bed after I arrived. When I shuffle into the kitchen, I find my mom in the sun-filled nook where she has a cozy seating area. Growing up, she would often sit here quietly in the mornings before we would all wake up and the daily chaos would begin.

"Case, chéri, come here baby!" she smiles widely when she sees me, opening her arms and enveloping me in one of her amazing mom hugs.

Sophie Radner-Armstrong grew up in America, but her family is French, and she spent every summer in France until she was in her mid-twenties. Her normal speaking voice doesn't hold even a trace of French accent, but occasionally, if she's extra tired or stressed, you can hear just a smidge. Because of my dad's job in politics, she always worked to not have an accent, not wanting to seem 'different'. She raised all of us to be Americans, but she always ensured we knew all about our French family history and traditions.

"Case, love, sit down. How are you doing, sweetie? Coffee?" she asks with a smile, indicating the French press she's using to top off her coffee mug.

"Yeah, thanks maman," I say, and when she places my mug in front of me, extra sweet, just how I like it, a warm feeling of belonging spreads through my chest. Suddenly I'm struck by a thought: I had the same warm feeling when I was with Matt. That sense of comfort and trust. Knowing I can be 100% myself, and I'm safe.

Mom looks at me, and right away she knows something's up. The woman misses nothing. "Tell me what's happening, baby," she smiles encouragingly, taking a sip of her own coffee.

I don't even hesitate. I lay it all out for her, starting with the night in Chicago and finishing with how I felt when I drove away from the cabin yesterday.

When I'm finished, she sits back in her chair and takes a long drink from her mug.

"So, it sounds like this Matthew is someone special, yes?"

"I don't think I've ever felt this way about another person. And that's scaring the living shit out of me. Because what if something happened and I lost him?" I shake my head. "It's just easier when you don't get attached to anyone, you know? I don't like being that vulnerable."

She nods slowly. "Case, I'm going to be honest, okay? I don't want you to feel hurt by anything I'm saying, okay?"

"Ooookay? I say, giving her a confused look.

"Case, when you were a little boy, you were always so cautious, whereas your brother Danny was always wild and fearless. The other kids all fell somewhere in the middle, but I always felt like you and Danny were like two sides of a coin. You two were so close, and you loved each other so much, but you were so very different. As much as I love both of you, I used to wish sometimes that you could each break off a small chunk of your personalities and trade them. Because I always worried you would miss out on things because you were so cautious, and that Danny would take a foolish risk and hurt himself."

"I know, maman, and look what happened to Danny. He took a risk, and he didn't come home!" I say sharply.

"I thought that way for a long time too, and I was so angry that he would take a foolish risk for no reason, just to chase the adrenaline. But it slowly dawned on me that I was wrong. I talked with all his friends who were with him that day, and many of his other friends as well. Every single one of them agreed Danny was the most safety conscious of everyone. They were all careful, but it was always Danny who would make sure the final checks were done on their equipment, made sure they always tested their avalanche beacons before every outing. They even said they would tease him about it." She smiles before taking another sip of coffee.

"Danny wasn't taking an unreasonable risk at all. He just wasn't letting his fear hold him back from doing what he wanted to do. He always made safe, smart decisions, minimizing the risk as much as possible, but he still experienced all the things he wanted to. What happened out there that day was just random chance. And I know to the depths of my soul that Danny was as well prepared as he could have possibly been. He did everything right, and we lost him anyway. But do you know what I realized, baby?"

I shake my head.

"It's not that he wasn't scared, he was, but he did what he wanted to do anyway. He prepared and tried to minimize the risks, but then he did the things he dreamed of doing. Your brother had some amazing experiences in his short life. And while I would give anything to have him back, it gives me comfort knowing that he lived his life to the very fullest."

I'm speechless for a few moments, processing what she's saying. I've never thought of Danny's life and death that way before.

"Sweetie, you're in your 40s now." My mom continues. "You've made a wonderful life for yourself, and I'm so proud of you. But I know you've held yourself back from things out of fear. I didn't used to worry so much about it, since you always seemed happy. But hearing how you talk about this Matthew... It's clear you want to be with him. But it sounds like you're letting your fear hold you back. And that worries me." She pauses to take a sip of coffee.

"If you both want to be together, if this will bring you happiness, then be brave, my love. Fight for it. If he's letting fear hold him back, you be brave enough for both of you. It's okay to be afraid. But do it anyway. Don't miss out on the possibility of something wonderful."

Chapter Twenty-Three

Matthew

After arriving home, I try to distract myself from missing Case, but after a few days, even thinking about work and brainstorming new game ideas isn't working.

It's still the dead week between Christmas and New Year's Eve where we keep the office closed because no one works during that time, anyway. I'm alone in my office, sitting at my desk, trying desperately to lose myself in work.

Hunter has been trying to get hold of me for the last couple of days, but I've been conveniently missing his calls and making excuses over text, telling him how busy I am trying to catch up. I know he won't believe me, but I'm not ready to explain why I'm such a mopey, grumpy fucker.

When the phone on my desk rings and I see that it's Michele calling, I know I'm busted. She rarely calls my office, but I've dodged one of her calls too, so she's determined to track me down.

I heave a sigh and answer the phone, knowing she's going to be annoyed with me. "Hey there," I say, picking up and trying to sound casual.

"Hey there," she says. "You've been hiding the last few days, hmm?"

"Well, I don't know about hiding. I've been busy catching up," I say weakly, but she doesn't buy it for one second.

"Matthew, I got a call from Hunter earlier today. He's concerned about you, worried you're avoiding him," she says with a tinge of recrimination in her voice.

"Hunter called you? Really?" I ask. *Shit.*

"Yup. He said but you've been avoiding him since you got home from the cabin."

Letting out a sigh. "Yeah, I'm fine. I'll call him later today. It's just been a weird few days."

"Matthew Cartwright, tell me what's going on," she says in her 'no-nonsense mom' voice, but it softens as she asks, "Are you okay, really? I was worried about you spending Christmas alone. I wish you would have flown out here to be with us."

"No, I'm okay, it's not that." I say. I hesitate for a moment before deciding to lay it all out for her. I guess this will be a test of the new friendship phase in our relationship. "I wasn't actually alone for Christmas. I- someone was at the cabin with me."

"Oh, really?" she says, and I can almost hear her eyebrows rising. "Okay, hon, you'd better fill me in. Just because we're not married anymore doesn't mean you get to stop being my best friend."

I laugh. She's always known how to make me feel better when the chips are down. I'm relieved she's not going to let me hide from our friendship.

"I hope you're sitting down, because some of this might surprise you," I say, and she laughs.

"Oh goody. Let me pour a glass of wine and get comfortable."

So, I confess to my ex-wife I'm not straight, but to my complete and utter disbelief, she doesn't even seem surprised.

"Matty, I suspected maybe you were curious. I never would have said anything to you about it. I didn't think you were even aware. But I'm so happy you've explored that part of you, honey."

I'm stunned into silence for a few moments. She suspected I might be into men? Even before I did? I shake my head and decide to blow past it. I simply don't have the energy to deal with all my questions about that.

So I tell her the rest of the story, starting with the night in Chicago, all the shit I've worked on in therapy, and ending with not being able to get Case out of my mind since we've been apart.

She blows out a soft whistle. "Wow, Matthew Cartwright, you have had a lot going on, haven't you? And it sounds to me like you've got some serious feelings for this guy."

"Mich, I have no idea how this happened. And what the actual fuck am I supposed to do? I mean, it's not like I can just leave the business and move to California on a whim. And he can't leave his position at the university, he's doing really important work there. I think we're just fucked, no matter how you look at it."

Michele is quiet for a moment before she clears her throat. "So, tell me something, Matthew. What is the reason, specifically, that you can't move there?"

I scoff. "Michele, you know why. I can't leave the business. It won't run itself. I need to be here."

"Mmm hmmm. But do you?" she says in a quiet voice. "Do you actually *need* to be there, or do you *want* to be there? It's a very convenient excuse for you to just keep doing the same thing you've been doing for the last twenty-five years."

"What? What do you mean? Of course, I need to be here. I mean.. But I want to be with Case.." my voice trails off.

"If you want to be with him, if that's what you truly want, you can make it happen, Matthew. You know as well as I do you don't have to be the one running the day-to-day ops at the company. Someone else could do that shit."

"Yeah.. I suppose you're right." I say.

"Listen, Matthew, I'm going to give you a little tough love here, okay?" she says, and I brace myself. She's never been one to mince words.

"Okay."

"You've spent your life putting that company ahead of everything and everyone else in your life. Now, don't get me wrong, that's a decision you and I made together, and ultimately, I'm completely fine with how we lived our lives. It was important to both of us to have the means to give our kids great educations, to take amazing trips and show them the world. And god knows, you and I both like our creature comforts. But we have enough now, more than enough. And you've given that company enough of your life. Let it go. Or at least don't let it hold you back."

I blow out a long breath, not exactly sure how to process what she's saying. "You're really not pulling any punches tonight, are you?"

"Matthew, honey, you know I'll always love you. You've been my best friend for far longer than we were married. We did a good job together, we raised three amazing people, and we had a good run as a married couple, but we were done. And now we both have this opportunity to lead a different life than the one we led together. I know you love the company, but you need to at least think about moving it down on your priority list. Case sounds like someone special. Don't let him pass you by without at least considering some changes."

I blow out another sigh. As she often does, Michele has managed to see through the layers of bullshit, and cut right to the heart of the matter.

"You make some good points."

"I know I do. I want what's best for you, you know that, right? I love you, my friend."

"I know. Thank you Michele. I love you too. Thanks for always telling me the truth, even when I don't want to hear it."

"You know I always will. Now, I want to you pack up your shit, go home, and pour yourself a nice Scotch. Maybe sit in the hot tub for a while. But think about what I said. Call me if you want to talk more, okay?"

"I will, thanks Michele. Say hi to the kids when you see them, right?"

"I will. Now go home, Matthew."

"I'm going," I say, smiling.

I pack away my laptop and hit the light switch in my office. Michele is right. I could hand off the day-to-day drudgery part of the company to someone else. Wasn't I just thinking that I'd love to do nothing but sit around daydreaming up new game ideas? Why the hell can't I do that? The only thing stopping me is me. The company will be just fine with someone else handling the minutiae. I'm not even at my house before I have a plan for what I'm going to do. The excitement that rolls through me thinking about it tells me it's the right decision. Now all I need to do is execute on the plan.

Chapter Twenty-Four

Case

Three days is about my limit when it comes to spending time at my parents' place when all of us are 'in residence', and this time I stayed nearly a week. I love all my siblings to death, but when we're all there, it's a lot. I was more than happy to drive away from them a couple of hours ago. We can be a rowdy bunch, and I'm looking forward to some quiet time.

The talk I had with my mom was helpful, although it took me a day or two to really absorb it. But when you strip away everything, I've made many decisions based on fear. Some of that is okay, but I don't want to miss a chance to have something with Matt. I don't know how well I'm going to deal with the way being in love makes me vulnerable, but that horse has left the barn. I love Matt, and I need to tell him. When I'm staying with my family, though, it can be hard to get time alone for a private phone call, and he said he's had a lot of catching up to do at work. We've talked and texted, but we haven't had any serious conversations yet. I plan to change that tonight.

Pulling into the garage of my townhome next to the beach, I get that warm feeling in my chest. I'm a California boy, through and through. I love it here, but I know that if being with Matt means I need to relocate, that will be okay. It's just geography. My home is with Matt. I just haven't figured out how to deal with the work issue yet. That part won't be easy, but I'm determined to find a way to make it work.

MATTHEW

I've been sitting in my rental car parked on the street outside Case's house in Carlsbad for long enough to feel like a stalker. I'm guessing he got away from his parents' house later than planned. I swear, I'll never complain about that little habit, though. If he had left his friend Reed's place earlier the morning he was supposed to go skiing with his friends, we would have never crossed paths again. So I'll happily spend the rest of my life being okay with his chronic lateness. And I do intend for it to be the rest of my life.

I've spent the last day and a half talking with Hunter about taking over more company operations, so I don't have to be around as much. He was floored when I told him I wanted to make him COO, and while I know he's ready for it, he's nervous.

I'm just changing things around so that I get to do more of what I want—which is work on the creative side of things. I want to come up with new ideas, and figure out how we can use new technologies to make games that can not only entertain, but educate.

My focus, though, the biggest reason for this change, is the man I just watched pull his white SUV into the garage of the beachfront townhome. He leaves the garage door open while he gets his bags out, and I climb out of my rental, watching him with a smile as I walk up his driveway. When I get close enough, I can hear him singing under his breath. It sounds like Harry Styles, which makes me laugh. He jumps and turns around quickly, his face lighting up when he sees me.

"Holy shit!" He drops the duffel bag he's holding, and we crash together like it's been months since we've seen each other, instead of only a few days.

"What are you doing here?" he asks breathlessly when we come up for air. I grin at him.

"I was in the neighborhood," I grin, and he rolls his eyes cheekily. "Let's go inside and I'll fill you in."

Case's home is stunning. It's on the beach in Carlsbad, a little coastal town about halfway between Los Angeles and San Diego. He has a huge patio off the front of his house, as well as a rooftop garden, making it easy to enjoy the stunning view of the ocean. His place is decorated simply, but it's welcoming and homey. While he makes us drinks in the kitchen, I wander around, checking things out. There's one photo I love. It's Case with what must be all his siblings, including Danny, on a ski trip. The photo shows them all with their jackets off, but still wearing ski pants and boots. Everyone's sunglasses are pushed up on their heads, and they all have brilliant smiles on their faces. The background is a stunning mountain vista, and everyone's laughing, arms around each other with rosy cheeks and big toothy grins. Just looking at the photo makes me smile.

Case steps up behind me while I'm looking at it. He hands me my drink and then presses up against me, his chest to my back, and with his free arm he encircles my waist, holding me close.

"I love this photo. You all look so happy."

Case rests his chin on my shoulder, looking at the photo, and I can hear the smile in his voice. "We were. That was the best trip. A couple of years before Danny died, we did a family trip and spent a week skiing at Whistler Mountain in BC. It's one of my best memories."

I nod, placing the photo back on the table, and turning to him. "That's a powerful reminder to do the things you want to do while you can. Don't put things off." I smile at him. "And that's kind of why I'm here. Let's sit outside?"

Outside, Case lights the fire table to ward off the cool, damp air starting to creep in from the ocean, and turns on a string of white Christmas lights. He sits back on the outdoor couch, one leg stretched out, and his other leg still on the ground. Then he pulls me into him and arranges us so I'm leaning against him with my back against his chest. He covers us with a cozy blanket and leans in to kiss my temple before letting out a quiet sigh. "I'm so fucking happy you're here," he says, and I can hear the smile in his voice.

"I am too," I say, taking a sip of my drink. "And the best thing is that I'm going to be able to stay for a while."

I can hear the confusion in his voice when he replies. "Not that I'm not thrilled by that idea, but how's that going to work? I thought you couldn't work remotely that often without things getting messed up."

"That's actually the best part," I say. I made a few big decisions over the last couple of days. And they affect both of us."

"What?" he says softly.

I shift so I can turn and see his face before responding. "I'm stepping back from the day to day running of the company. I've given Hunter the job and I'm going to focus more on the creative side of things. Which means I don't have to be in the office as often."

"You did?" Case's eyes are round with surprise, the corners of his mouth twitching slightly as if he's holding back a smile.

I nod. "I did. Michele called me a couple of days ago, and she gave me shit about putting the company at the top of my priority list. I was all twisted in knots about you, and what to do about us, and she just cut through all the bullshit and told me to pull my head out of my ass and go get you. She made me see that if I want this chapter of my life to turn out differently than the last one, I need to change my priorities."

"Oh my god," he says, allowing the smile to take over his face. "Matt, that's fucking amazing. So, you'll be able to spend more time here? With me?" he looks like a little kid who's just been promised a puppy.

I nod. "I think I would have made this decision even if we weren't together. I was even thinking about it before you arrived at the cabin, but just hadn't allowed myself to see that I could actually make it happen. Michele just reminded me."

Case laughs. "It sounds like I owe Michele a big thank you."

"Possibly." I smile. "But, I just want to make sure for the record–is this okay with you? I didn't discuss it with you first, and if you're more comfortable taking things slowly, I don't have to-"

Case stops me by leaning forward and planting a kiss on my mouth. It's a sweet, almost chaste kiss, but it holds all kinds of promises. "I want you here. I want you here all the time," he whispers, gently tracing the curve of my jaw with his fingers. "I talked to my mom about you. She said something similar to me about pulling my head out of my ass. She clued me into the fact that I've allowed fear to hold me back from a lot of things, especially since Danny's death. But I'm ready to stop letting fear make my decisions." He clears his throat, and my grip tightens on his hand.

"I'm scared, but I realized the other night that trying to push you away isn't going to help me, anyway. It's too late for that. I love you, Matt. I'm completely in love with you, and it's scary, and perfect and exciting, and I.. I just love you. I'm not going to let fear take that away from us."

Tears fill my eyes as I lunge at him, crushing our mouths together in a kiss that feels like forever. We cling to each other, letting our mouths explore and taste and savor each other. Finally, we have to break apart for air, and I cling to him gasping. His eyes are bright as we smile at each other. "I love you too, Case. I love you so much I hardly believe it. I never thought I'd be in love again, and everything about us is different than what I've known before, and it's so much better than I could have ever imagined."

He shuts off my excited babbling with another kiss, and when he pulls back, he's laughing. "Let's take this celebration to the bedroom, Mister Cartwright. I have a few things I want to do that will show you exactly how much I love you."

After Case shuts down the fire, and we move to the bedroom, a powerful feeling of rightness settles over me again. Similar to the way I felt that first afternoon at the cabin. I know, right down to the marrow of my bones, that I'm exactly where I'm supposed to be. I'm with Case. I'm home.

Epilogue

Christmas Eve, Two Years Later

CASE

"Hey, come check this out," I call over my shoulder to Matt, who's sitting on the couch just inside the sliding glass doors that open onto our patio. He sets down his book and gets up, closely followed by our rescue mutt, Lou. He slides the glass door open enough so they can step onto the big deck at the back of our cabin tucked away in the Rocky Mountains. He stands beside me at the railing and lets out a soft gasp as he takes in the unbelievable show happening in the sky above us: bright greens and blues dancing and waving across the sky. It's the first time I've ever seen the Northern Lights so clearly.

This is the first year we've been celebrating Christmas at our own mountain cabin. It's hard to believe the changes we've been through in the last couple of years, but I can honestly say they have been the happiest years of my life.

"Oh my god, it's so beautiful," Matt breathes, his face turned up to the sky as he watches the lights move and undulate above us. I, on the other hand, can't seem to tear my eyes off him. Two years later and I'm still fascinated by how beautiful he is to me. His dark brown eyes are shining with excitement, and when I put my hand on the small of his back, not able to keep myself from touching him, he turns to me, and I can see the love in them.

After we decided to go all in on our relationship, it wasn't long before Matt moved down to Carlsbad with me. We keep his home in Seattle, as we spend a lot of time there when Matt needs to be in the office or when I meet with Penn at his shelter, who is now contributing even more to our research project. Matt's kids and Michele also use the house when they're on the west coast, so it gets plenty of use.

This cabin is something we decided to do very shortly after we got together. It just took us a long time to find the right place. Since we're in California most of the time now, we decided the location didn't have to be within easy driving distance of Seattle, it just had to be close to an airport. We found this place online less than a year ago, and once we realized it's an easy drive from the airport in Calgary, Alberta, we knew this was the place. It needed some renovations, which were finished a couple of weeks ago. We arrived last week, and we're going to be here until the end of January. We'll have family and other have visitors for several weekends, but we're both perfectly happy to settle in and exist in our own little bubble by ourselves, recapturing some of the same magic from those first days at a different mountain cabin.

As we stand watching the lights, I move so I'm standing behind him, my arms around his waist, loving the way he melts back into me, trusting I'm there to hold him up. "This is incredible, right?" he murmurs, gently running his fingers over my hands clasped over his abdomen.

"So incredible," I whisper back to him, dragging my nose along the tendons of his neck and nibbling on his earlobe.

We stand at the railing for a long time, just watching the sky, but eventually the lights start to fade, and Lou starts to whine–his way of telling us it's time for bed. Spoiled mutt.

I shut off the fire table and the string lights and follow Matt into the house, smiling when my gaze lands on the Christmas gift he gave me today.

It's a beautiful print on canvas of my favorite family picture. The one with all my siblings during our last ski vacation together before Danny died.

I was moved to tears when I opened it. Matt did such a good job of keeping it a secret. I don't know how he managed to slip the old photo out of the house without me noticing, but he did, and I'm so happy. It's perfect here in our mountain getaway, close to several world-class ski hills. I can't wait to show my family when they get here in a few days.

I stop in the kitchen on my way to the bedroom, just to putter for a few minutes and bask in the perfection of this place. We've made a tradition of tomato soup and grilled cheese sandwiches as our Christmas Eve dinner, and it's been perfect. I can't believe how happy this life has made me, and I'm so thankful I didn't let fear stop me from going after the best thing that's ever happened to me.

MATTHEW

I let Lou out to do his business before heading back upstairs to the main floor of the house where the living room and our bedroom is. I can hear Case puttering around in the kitchen so as soon as I brush my teeth I grab the little black box I have hidden in one of my drawers, and snuggle into bed. I smile, as I always do, when I see our gay Santa-bear sheets. Hunter's husband, Penn, was able to tell us where he got them. Apparently, they're quite popular with a certain crowd.

A few minutes later, Case comes into the room, and he stops to give Lou a scratch before he heads into the bathroom. He's back quickly, taking a running jump from the door of the bathroom and landing on the bed, nearly bouncing me right off it. We're both laughing as he grabs me, pulling me roughly to him and then rolling so he's on top of me, pressing me into the soft sheets.

He hooks his arms under my shoulders, pressing our chests together and gives me a long, slow kiss that takes my breath away.

"Merry Christmas, Mister Cartwright," he murmurs as he grazes his nose along my jawline.

"Mmmm. Merry Christmas to you, Mister Armstrong," I reply, and we share a smile that I swear to god could light up a small town. I never in my life dreamed I could be so happy. I had always believed contentment was the goal. I always sort of assumed when people said they were happy, what they really meant was that they were content with their lives, because who's *actually* happy all the time?. But these last three years have shown me how wrong I was. Case lights up my life in a way no one else ever has.

My company continues to thrive with Hunter at the helm. I've been able to spend my time coming up with a few new creative concepts and it's been fun to experiment with them. But honestly, I'd be happy doing nothing but living in our home with Case, reading books and walking the dog on the beach every day. I've found I don't miss work at all, which was a huge surprise, given it was the center of my life for so long. But even my kids have remarked that I seem like a different person than the dad they knew growing up. They all love Case, and are truly happy for me. Michele has been our biggest cheerleader, and she's struck up a close friendship with Case's mom, Sophie.

I take a deep breath, and using all my strength I roll Case off me, and turn us so he's on his back while I'm straddling him. He laughs at me and runs his hands up and down my thighs. "Mmm, someone's feeling a little bossy tonight?" he says with an evil smile. I laugh, leaning forward to kiss him, but pulling back before the kiss deepens into more.

Case's eyes are twinkling as he grins up at me. He knows me so well, he knows I've got something up my sleeve.

"Okay, my love, what's going on? You look like the cat that ate the canary up there."

"Well, I have a little surprise for you," I smile at him, and before he can even make a saucy remark about it, I stun him by whipping out the little black velvet box and opening it to show him the two platinum bands nested inside.

"What!" he gasps, his eyes round as saucers.

"So I had a big speech all planned out for this," I say in a soft voice. "But it just didn't feel like us. You know how much I love you, and I hope I tell you enough how happy you make me." Case starts to say something, but I place a finger to his lips "Shhh–my turn first. You'll get your chance in a minute." I grin at him as he rolls his eyes.

"So, instead of trying to think up a big speech, I decided to do this in bed, since it's kind of where this whole thing started. I love you Case, more than you can even imagine, and I hate to think of what my life would be like if you hadn't come up to my table that night in Chicago. I might never have acknowledged this side of myself, and fucking hell would I have missed out." I grin.

Case's eyes are filled with tears as he looks up at me, but the smile on his face is pure light. "So, what you're saying is that you're putting a ring on it. Locking me down, huh?"

I snort with laughter. "Absolutely. I don't want anyone else horning in on this action. You're all mine, baby."

He sits up and pulls me against him, giving me a huge hug. "All yours. Sometimes I still can't believe we ended up together. I mean, what are the chances, right? I don't usually believe in fate, as you know, but when it comes to us...." He shakes his head, his tears spilling over. "Of course I'll marry you, Matthew Cartwright. There's nothing else in the world I want more."

Thanks so much for reading An Unexpected Gift. I hope you loved Case & Matt's story.

Have you read all the Hot Dam Homes books? _From The Ground Up_ is Mason & Jackson's steamy, celebrity & blue collar guy story.

https://mybook.to/ftgu

In _When The Walls Come Down_ Dylan & Reed get their unlikely, but worth-the-wait happily ever after.

https://mybook.to/wwcd

All books are available in Kindle Unlimited.

You'll love my new _Seattle Sasquatch Hockey_ series.

Book One: _Rylan_ is available at

https://mybook.to/rylan

Keep up with all Harper Robson's news & info on sales and more goodies by signing up for the VIP newsletter at
https://www.subscribepage.com/harpernewsletter

SEATTLE SASQUATCH HOCKEY

M/M HOCKEY ROMANCE

The Seattle Sasquatch

The Seattle Sasquatch took the NHL by storm, shocking the hockey world by winning the Stanley Cup in their inaugural season. But just a couple of years later, the team is grappling with the pressure of staying on top in a cutthroat league. As egos clash and tensions reach a boiling point, their once-unbreakable bonds are put to the ultimate test.

At the heart of the storm is team captain Rylan Collings, who led the Sasquatch to their first heart-stopping championship, but is now haunted by his own personal demons and carries the weight of his team's struggles on his shoulders.

In net, Louis Tremblay, the cheeky, mischievous goaltender, must contend with a younger hotshot who's gunning for the number one job.

Other players, their new Coach, and General Manager Carson Wells must all navigate their own struggles and wrestle with secrets, all while trying to lead this talented but troubled team back to the summit of the hockey world.

Will the Sasquatch buckle under the pressure, leaving team ownership with no choice but to break up their beloved squad? Or will they find the resilience to conquer personal demons, defy expectations, and hoist the Cup again?

Each book in the series is a steamy, standalone romance.

Rylan: Seattle Sasquatch Book 1

https://mybook.to/rylan

Rylan

One hot night with my teammate threatens to expose my secret and end my career.

I've spent my entire hockey career hiding who I really am. Between trying to lead my struggling team, dealing with an alcoholic father, and living in the shadow of my brother's legacy, my life feels like one endless fight. The last thing I need is for anyone to discover my secret. Then Jamie Pirelli arrives—young, talented, and openly queer. He sees through all my walls, and suddenly everything I've built is at risk.

Jamie

I'm more than just the first openly bisexual player in the league.

A lot more. But after a disastrous start to my pro hockey career in Florida, Seattle is my last chance to prove it. I can't afford any more scandals, but the chemistry between me and my deep-in-the-closet captain is impossible to ignore. Our connection on the ice is what hockey legends are made of.

Off the ice? That's a different game altogether.

Rylan is a high-stakes hockey romance between the team captain with loads of baggage and the younger superstar struggling to be taken seriously. An impossible-to-resist forbidden relationship between a wounded control freak with a tragic backstory and a sunshiny free spirit with a tarnished reputation.

Sign Up for Harper's Newsletter for all the updates on the Sasquatch and lots more.

https://www.subscribepage.com/harperbackmatter

Acknowledgments

Thank you so much for reading *An Unexpected Gift*. This project grew from a short story into a full novel, and then shrank back down into a long-ish novella. It was fun to write, but it was also a fantastic learning experience (I won't bore you with those details).

For me, 2022 will always be special because it was the year I published my first book. When I realized there are people out there who actually want to read the stories I make up in my head, it was quite a revelation, and I couldn't be more grateful.

My biggest thanks always go to my friend Jeris Jean, without whom I would have never believed I could write a book. There's a lot of power in having someone quietly believe you're capable of doing something, even when that something is hard.

This year I also got to be part of an anthology *(Cruising)* and that group of talented authors turned into an amazing group of friends. Duckie Mack, Matthew Dante, Garry Michael, Michael Robert, Michaela Cole, LD Blakely, S. Legend, and of course, Jeris Jean, thank you so much for all the support, information and laughter you've given so freely this year. I'm not sure I'd be able to do this without you, so you're stuck with me now!

My coven of mom-friends in Seattle, you know who you are, and my best girl, Carrie, I love you all so much. Our ongoing text threads keep me sane and laughing more days than I can count and I don't know what I would do without you guys.

This book took more time away from my family than my other books have (see *learning experience* above) so thank you to my husband, my two boys, and my two dogs who drive me insane but whom I love more than anything.

And finally, *(*cue the orchestra playing me off the stage)* I'm so grateful to you, dear reader. I'm having so much fun doing this writing thing, and you enjoying the books and the characters I come up with makes me happier than I could have imagined!

I have big plans for 2023, including Book 3 and possibly Book 4 of the Hot Dam Homes series, as well as something brand new I'm excited about. Keep an eye on my newsletter and social media for more info. You can also email me anytime, at harper@harperro bson.com. I'd love to hear from you.

Love & light,

Harper

xox

December 2022

Chilliwack, BC

The Getaways Series

Making Waves: Hunter & Penn https://myboo
k.to/makingwaves

Making Waves Audiobook: Narrated by Kevin
Earlywine & Cole Michael Kurcz
available at shop.harperrobson.com

Love After Love: Martin & Jesse (a Getaways
Novella) https://mybook.to/loveafterlove

The Seattle Sasquatch Series

Rylan: Book One https://mybook.to/rylan
Louis: Book Two (2025) https://mybook.to/lou
Austin: Book Three (2025)
Carson: Book Four (2026)
Part of the *Seattle Sasquatch* World

The Night Before: Aleks & Ben https://mybook.to
/thenightbefore
A *Seattle Sasquatch Hockey* Christmas Prequel Novel

**All books are available on Amazon and in
Kindle Unlimited (unless otherwise noted)**

ALL ABOUT HARPER ROBSON

Harper Robson grew up dreaming about being a writer someday. That someday didn't arrive until she was in her mid-forties–but better late than never! While traveling that long and winding road, she worked in marketing, software development, the oil & gas industry and spent more than a decade as a stay-home mom. She grew up in Vancouver, BC, but feels most at home in the leafy green suburbs of Seattle, Washington. In 2023, Harper and her clan pulled up stakes and headed south to live in San Diego, California. She was certain she'd miss the rainy, gray days of the Pacific Northwest, but it turns out regular doses of sunshine and palm trees are pretty easy to get used to, and San Diego feels more like home every day.

She's a mom to two teenaged boys and an adorable but naughty yellow Labrador Retriever. Her husband works in the tech industry and he makes her laugh every single day.

A true PNW girl, Harper loves the rain but is always planning her next beach vacation. Her favorite things include road trips, classic rock, the Seattle Kraken, her dogs, and drinking champagne for no reason at all.

She would love to hear from you anytime! Email her at harper@harperrobson.com

Visit harperrobson.com and sign up for the Newsletter

Let's Connect!

The best way to keep up with all things Harper is to sign up for the VIP Newsletter:
https://www.subscribepage.com/harpernewsletter

Bluesky: @harperrobsonauthor.bsky.social
Facebook: Harper Robson
Instagram: @harperrobsonauthor
BookBub: @harperrobsonauthor
Facebook Group: Harper's Heartbreakers: https://www.facebook.com/groups/harpersheartbreakers

Goodreads:

https://www.goodreads.com/author/show/2228446

9.Harper_Robson

Amazon Author Page

https://www.amazon.com/author/harperrobson

Website: www.harperrobson.com

Get Your Free Book!

A Clean Slate

Head over to

www.subscribepage.com/harperbackmatter

to sign up for my VIP newsletter. You'll receive a free copy of *A Clean Slate,* Eric and Drew's steamy, age-gap love story.

Eric

I've been dealing with a chronic illness since I was nine years old, and, believe me, it's a drag. Being a Type 1 diabetic affects every relationship in my life, from my parents all the way through the guys I date. After getting unceremoniously dumped because of it,

I've decided that romantic relationships aren't in the cards for me. The last thing I want is to be a burden on anyone. But when my best friend drags me to a weekend memorial for his grandmother and I meet his uncle, I start to wonder if he means it when he tells me I could never be a burden.

Drew

Being a single, gay man in New York city and making a decent living as a writer isn't a bad gig. But after the end of a long-term relationship, I'm at a crossroads. I can stay here and continue on with life as I know it, or I can take this opportunity to make a big change and start over in a new place. I've spent my entire adult life resisting change, but when I travel across the country for my mother's memorial weekend, I meet someone who makes me think that jumping in with both feet might not be the worst decision. The problem is, he's my nephew's best friend, and he's half my age.

A Clean Slate is a steamy, age-gap romance featuring a New York City-based writer and a West Coast

Ph.D student who probably shouldn't fit together, but somehow do.